# *Sing* Our Bones EternaL

Kacey Rayburn

*Sing Our Bones Eternal*


Published by House of Soul Cakes
First Edition

Cover Art: Chloe Coblentz ("Haunted Chloe")
Cartographer: J.C. Greening
Printed in the United States of America

*Thematic material includes psychological horror, violence, abuse, blood, animal sacrifice, and sex between consenting partners.*

# Dedication

For all my ancestors, the quick and the dead.

For Ruth and Debbie, the best mirror-keepers I've ever known.

And for James, my eternal wulver.

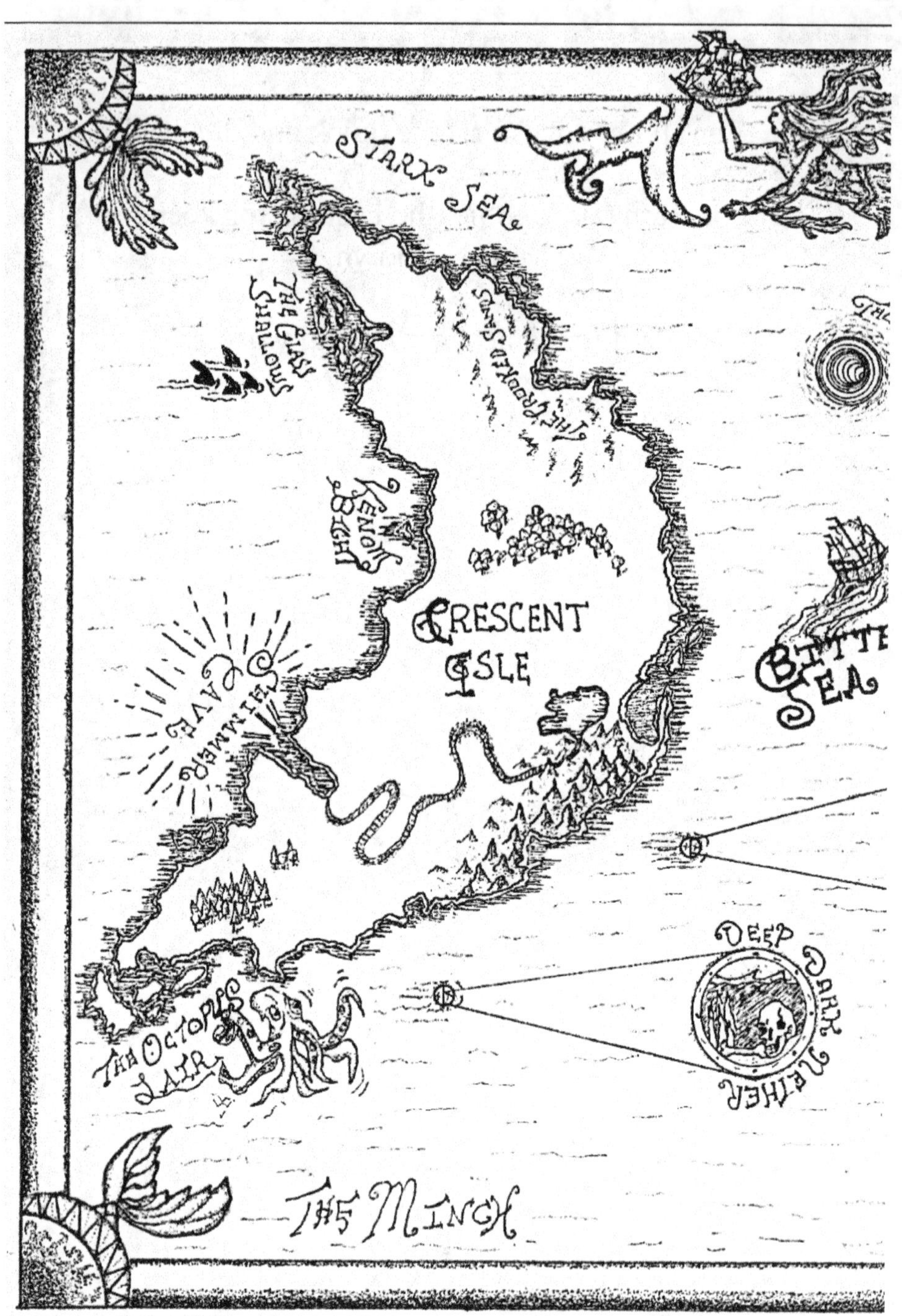

STARX SEA
THE GLASS SHALLOWS
THE CROOKED SANDS
KENOLL BIGHT
CRESCENT ISLE
SHIMMER CAVE
THE OCTOPUS LAIR
DEEP DARK NETHER
THE MINCH

WULVER COVE
CAULDRON
HERE THERE BE DRAGONS
THE PEEKABOOS
SEA CAVES
TEA HOUSE
HIDEY POOLS
HOURGLASS ISLE
HUTCH
BLACKHOUSE
N
SING OUR BONES ETERNAL
HALL OF MIRRORS
THE WEEP
NARROWS
BRITTLE FOREST
FALLOW POINT
BRIGHT SEA

# 1

## The Mermaid Chorus

Some souls are born so hungry they enter the world a bloody, hissing mess. Fangs bared, they feast on mother meat, tender-pink, but it's not enough. Craving more, they consume the world around them, sparing only what's out of reach: a sky of lonely stars, a silver-bellied moon, and the deep salt sea.

# 2

# The Mermaid Chorus

Long ago, when the sea was young, there was a hungry mermaid named Kilda. She was an exquisite creature from head to tail, with honey-blonde curls, almond eyes, long lashes, and pearls in her hair. On her fifteenth birthday, Kilda rose above the salt and scratched the skin of the sea. She finned for Crescent Isle, following the cold light of the moon. With a splash, she flopped onto the black sand and fell into a deep sleep.

At dawn, Kilda woke and tasted the fruits of the earth. She crushed berries between her fangs and painted her lips with their blood. She gorged on shiny apples and juicy lobsters. She lolled on The Crooked Sands, gazing up at the ghost-clear sky. Life on land was splendid, for there was no veil of water to obscure her vision.

The seasons lived and died, each blossoming until it wilted. Many a long day Kilda spent on Crescent Isle, exploring every nook and cranny. Her body became a refuge for many creatures. Shrimp burrowed between her scales; petrels nested in her wild hair.

It was all so beautiful – until Kilda grew restless. The isle she once loved became the bane of her existence. She despised the dirty shrimp between her scales and the cold moon with its crooked spine. Crescent Isle wasn't even an isle. It was more of a sandspit, really.

Tempted by new wonders, Kilda set her sights on the neighboring isle. For seven hundred and seventy moons, Kilda swam to Hourglass Isle. She hid behind the sunbaked rocks, her keen eyes floating on the surf. Sly as a devilfish, she watched the wulvers as they lugged their nets along the shore and sang their shanties around the fire.

The wulvers were handsome indeed, dressed in salt and pepper fur, with broad shoulders and rippling muscles, but Kilda fancied the fallows. Her heart hammered as they pranced along the windswept shore. Each time she saw one, she swam closer than before. They always greeted her with big doe eyes and bone-white antlers, but before she could utter a word, they dashed back to The Brittle Forest.

Every night in her oyster bed, Kilda dreamt of the fallows. She followed them into the mist as they led her deep into The Brittle Forest. Kilda watched with delight as they pranced around a crackling fire, their antlers smearing in the shadows. She sat under a canopy of leaves and listened to the owls hooting in the pine trees.

When Kilda awoke from her dreams, she felt a stab of jealousy. The wulvers weren't bound to the sea, and the fallows could come and go as they pleased. It wasn't fair. Kilda loathed her soggy lungs and her clumsy tail. Of all the eternals she could've been, a mermaid was the lowliest. To ease her pain, she told herself glorious stories.

*I'm better than my sisters. I belong above the salt. I deserve the fresh blue sky, a cloud-soaked throne, and the sweat of the sun. I deserve a herd of loyal fallows to dance around me and a crown of antlers bursting berry-red. I deserve an altar of smoke curling in my name. If only I could shake off these odious scales. If only I could rip the human heart from my chest, then I could become a god and rule Hourglass Isle.*

A faint whisper caressed her ears: *Hourglass Isle is yours*. But it was only the wind rustling through the leaves; such was the dangerous nature of hunger, causing creatures to mistake the crunch of grass for the crackle of bacon.

One starry night, Kilda refused to sleep in her oyster bed. She rose above the salt instead. With heavy eyes, she ordered a crab to pinch her if she fell asleep.

A pinch and a half later, Kilda snapped to attention and scoured the shoreline. There, straight ahead, was a handsome fallow. Kilda finned her way to the water's edge and followed him. She crawled along a stretch of black sand, squeezing her body between the slippery rocks. Muscles aching, she ascended a steep hill that gave way to a clearing. By the time Kilda reached the top, her arms and her tail burned red-hot.

Overhead, a rowan tree blazed with berries. Entranced, Kilda stopped and stared at the herd of fallows prancing around it. With her last ounce of strength, she slithered over a carpet of crimson and gold leaves until she reached the rowan tree. The fallows bowed before her, pricking her with their antlers.

Hissing with pleasure, Kilda threw her arms around the rowan tree and pledged her allegiance to the land. She sang for the last time, a melody of blood and sand.

In one fell swoop, the rowan tree thrust its branches through her heart. All through the night, Kilda writhed in pain as the rowan tree devoured her. Her tail hardened to wood and her scales to bark. The ground absorbed her dark little magic as her poison spread throughout Hourglass Isle.

# 3

## Senga

There's a crack in the roof above my bed. My father put it there, perfect for peeking. I'm a thing to be watched when I sleep, when the candles burn low, and I undress to skin and bones. When I touch my tender parts under the sheets.

I feel eyes on me, dragging along my skin, eyes that belong to my uncle. I hate the way Gunn looks at me, all teeth and tongue, hungry enough to eat me.

When it rains, I dream. My bed is a rock and my room is the sea, waves rolling around me. I'm a sad sort of happy in this drowsy state, a bundle of nerves and a curl of limbs, sweaty hair sticking to my neck. I feel it coming, all wind and rain. I see it so clearly – the dream staring back at me before the tide carries it away.

I'm sitting on a cold rock, stitching my legs together. I feel the poke of the needle, the pull of the thread, my fingers slick with blood. I rub my tailbone, tracing fresh blooms of silver scales. The sky is broken, cracked open like an egg. Lightning strikes through a ring of fog. A waterspout spins around me. The storm is here, ready to swallow me whole, but I'm only half-afraid.

At the pink of dawn, I jolt awake. A ray of light licks me, washing away the dream. Familiar noises creep through the cracked roof: the crunch of my father's boots and the squeak of the latch. Nothing ever changes. The air still reeks of rancid meat, and Gunn lazes by the hearth guzzling mead.

I peek under the blanket, searching for bloody stitches, but my legs are smooth and clean. I hold my breath, giving my lungs a good stretch, while delicious pain swims through me. The mermaids are singing again, their voices knife-sharp – sharp enough to draw blood from my ears.

The land is never quiet here. There's a curse in every crevice, a trill in every tree. Sheep bleat in the meadow. Whales click in the sea. Lochs and rivers splash. The wind strums the thistles into dazzling little harps. Even the rocks snarl with song, for the earth remembers what my ancestors have done.

The past isn't gone. It's always here, nipping at my heels. Rumor has it my father is a wicked bluebeard from The Minch. When I ask him where he's from, he doesn't give me a straight answer. He just flashes his hook of a smile and says he's a bag of mystery.

We live on Hourglass Isle, surrounded by The Bitter Sea. And bitter it is, for it's never felt like home to me. Best I can figure, we're a dozen leagues north of Scotland, but it's hard to tell because I've never been on the mainland. I've never seen a map, either. My father forbids many things, maps and harps to name a few.

*Harps*. The very word casts a spell on me, hurling me back in time.

Time is slippery on Hourglass Isle, or perhaps it's just slippery for me. Fear has a way of warping time, bending it until it breaks. Something bad happens, and the ground splits beneath me. Memories scatter and splash into the sea, leaving behind a chain of isles. Here's the present, thin and jagged. There's the past, long and crooked. And everything in between.

How easily I swim from now to *then*: to the day my father took the harp away.

It's warm outside, not a cloud in the sky. My mother and I sit under the oak tree, the ground still damp with dewdrops. She wears a crown of fairy bells, her white gown fluttering in the breeze. Her hair is a blend of blood and earth, a rich mahogany gleaming in the sun. I scoot closer, savoring the smell of cinnamon on her skin.

Angel-pretty, she plucks her harp. I crave her attention, but her gaze lingers on the horizon. Perhaps she's searching for something she lost long ago, like her voice, a bitter root pulled before its time. My mother loves nothing more than to hear me sing. With an eager nod, she encourages me. I purse my lips in song and feel her moving through me, strumming the strings of my heart.

But something bad is coming. The nape of my neck tells me so, its tiny hairs standing on end. I cast my mother a worried glance. She forces a smile, her amber eyes warm as toast.

The front door squeals open, giving way to my father. He's built like a bull: short, stout, and full of thunder. He stomps his hoof-feet into the ground and scolds my mother for playing the harp. Then, with a wild snort, he charges at us.

Fear pulses through me, blurring my vision. In this moment, my father is not a man but a beast, with a mangy beard and a jumble of teeth. My mother springs to her feet, shielding me from my father. She bows before him, clasping her hands together. She doesn't know it, but she's teaching me something very important: my father is a god, and we must worship him. My mother continues groveling, kissing his feet in contrition.

But her apology only incenses my father more. He lunges at her, knocking her to the ground. He could stop right now, but he doesn't. My father has an insatiable soul, always wanting more. He yanks my mother by the hair and strikes her jaw. I cringe as bones crunch and teeth crack. My mother goes limp in his arms, blood spilling from her mouth.

Instinctively, I reach for her, but my father shoves me away. With a wild snort, he tosses my mother aside and guts her harp like a whale. When he finishes, he sets his sights on me, his eyes boring through my skin. I try to run away, but my feet are pinned to the ground. I cower down, biting back tears.

My father grabs me, his hands eating my neck. For a beat, he lets up, only to raise the harp strings over his head. I feel a sudden gust of wind, followed by the lash of strings. Blood rolls down my back; it hurts so badly I can hardly breathe.

How quickly things change. The harp is a weapon now, and I must endure the pain. Whether it's past or present, I'm always afraid of my father.

He's the lump in my throat, the stone I can't swallow.

But still, I feign he loves me. I imagine us rising from the hot breath of the earth, soaring above the salt until we crumble into stardust. I imagine his hands mending the lashes on my back, his tears sponging away my scars.

For what little I know of my father, I know even less of my mother. She bakes and sews like most mothers, but she never says a word. When she tries to speak, nothing comes out but a gurgle. The only remnants of who she used to be are a stack of music tomes with singed pages and several jars of tulip cream, which she lathers on her throat to ease her pain.

Every morning, I gaze into the mirror, searching for a piece of my mother, but her hair is thorn-bitten while mine is rose-red, and my eyes aren't warm as fire; they're cold as ice. The only features we share are heart-shaped faces and a smattering of freckles.

My father has been wary of me since the day I was born with a slimy caul on my head. He was ready to toss me over the sea cliffs and try again for another child, but my mother wouldn't hear of it. She stole me away to Wulver Cove and nursed me in the dim light of the sea caves. She suckled me until I looked like a normal child, until my eyes were clear as rain and my hair was fuzzy red, then she brought me back home to the castle.

*Oh, the castle.* The very thought of it wrenches my heart.

The castle was destroyed before I could form any memory of it, but I know I was born there, high above the salt. High enough to smell the copper bells tolling from sunrise to sunset on the day I came into this world.

I wasn't born beside a crackling fire in my mother's splendid bedchamber. Rather, I took my first breath in the dusty turret so my grandmother's ghost could witness the tender occasion. I don't remember anything about my grandmother, but I do remember my grandfather's black eyes and peculiar whiskers and the sealskin pouch he wore close to his heart.

My father says there's no use in crying over spilled milk. The Blackhouse is our home now, and we're not to speak of the castle. I wish it felt like home, but it doesn't. The Blackhouse was built on blood-soaked ground, spit together with the bones and ashes of my grandfather. There's no chimney inside, so the smoke hangs thick as a blanket. The cracked roof above my bed leaves me at the mercy of the wind and the rain. I may as well be living outside among the hawthorns and the fairies.

My aunt Lorna and uncle Gunn live with us. Their bedchamber is glorious, dressed in oak wood and velvet drapes, bright with candelabras and gilded mirrors. Despite such grandeur, Lorna still misses the castle. She's too stubborn to admit it, but I know she does. When the mood strikes her, she wears her skin inside out, her black heart breaking. On such days, it's best to leave her alone so she can ride her pony along the sea cliffs, her butter-blonde hair flying in the wind.

I try to understand Lorna, but she's not cut from the same cloth as my mother. Lorna hates singing and cooking. She has a penchant for pomp and frill, and she takes great pleasure in causing pain. If it weren't for Kilda's dark little magic, Lorna never would've agreed to live in The Blackhouse.

Last summer, I asked Lorna what *dark little magic* was, and she said it was Kilda's gift to our family. Lorna promised me I'd become a god if I made sacrifices like the other women in our family. My grandmother gave her life. Lorna gave up the castle. My mother gave up her voice.

And I must give up Ivor.

Ivor is the only person in this world I trust. If I ever lost him, my heart would surely break. Not to mention, I don't have any interest in godhood. I don't even believe in gods, at least not in the way my family does. Of course, I'd never tell them as much because they'd leave me to perish in The Brittle Forest with the unfortunate fallows.

Kilda's dark little magic may be a gift to our family, but it's a curse for the landies. While they beg and borrow for a bushel of corn and a drop of honey, we have everything we could ever want. On an isle of rag and bone, we have a herd of sheep and a cove full of hake. We feast on lamb stew, raspberry buns, and tea cakes soaked in butter. We drink sweet wine and spiced mead from silver horns. We ride the finest carts and ponies. We wear velvet gowns, lace skirts and blouses, shiny boots, and woolly socks and sweaters. We have weather-proof luggers, lethal weapons, and a cabinet full of herbs and poisons.

Sometimes, the landies come to us and beg for a morsel. With gloomy eyes and growling bellies, they plead for milk, lamb, and hake. After my father gives them barely enough to satisfy their hunger, they bow before him and bless him for feeding their children.

On occasion, I've heard the landies whispering to each other at the teahouse. They think I have the world on a silver platter, but there's more to life than fancy skirts and fine ponies.

Houses are husks, scratches in time, each one keeping secrets. The landies don't know what's lurking inside The Blackhouse, but I do, and it's far from luxurious. If only they knew the truth. I can't talk to anybody, not even my own mother, for she drools and garbles like a wild animal. The walls are deathly grey, caked in soot and ashes. The smoke dizzies me every night as try to sleep, my lungs a bright burn in the dark.

Chattering away, the landies live to see another day, surviving on tea and crumbs while my coffer overflows. I don't blame them for hating me and my family, but their gossip still hurts me.

*I think the bluebeards struck a deal with Kilda. How else could they have captured our isle and destroyed Lord Goldie and his castle? Now Hourglass Isle is soaked in blood, and we're starving.*

*Did you know that Warr took Twila against her will? She never wanted to marry him, let alone give birth to his daughter. As innocent as Senga seems, she can't be trusted, not with Warr's blood in her veins. She's still a bluebeard, and bluebeards are rotten to the core.*

Amid their hot whispers, I nearly jump on the table and shout. I want to defend my honor, but my efforts are futile. Nothing I say ever seems to matter. As far as the landies are concerned, I'm a heathen with sin-red hair and emerald eyes deep enough to drown in.

# 4

## Senga

On the fringes of light, I reach for the sun, but she eludes me. On a wing and a prayer, I drag myself out of bed and savor a bowl of porridge. My father is thick with mischief this morning; his footsteps echo in The Hutch underground. The very word – *hutch* – sends a chill down my spine.

I sweep past Gunn before he can catch hold of me and busy myself with chores outside. I scry the clouds in the dismal sky, but I find no answers. I don't even find an omen, good or bad. They're just clouds, puffs of nothing, grey and heavy. I feed the ponies and brush their manes, but I don't enjoy it, not the way I did when I was younger. The ponies are skittish around me; even *they* think I'm a wicked bluebeard.

I lift my eyes to the northern mountains, admiring them in all their ghostly glory. I long to know what lies beyond The Peekaboos, but they're always dipped in a halo of drizzling rain, looking bleak and ominous. Perhaps the edge of the world is waiting for me. Nature keeps many secrets, just like my family.

The bluebeards may be ruthless, but we live on the prettiest part of Hourglass Isle. If a traveler stood on a nearby hill, he'd see an impossibly tall blackhouse, perched on a windswept bluff. He'd see a tumble of stones hemmed in by the rolling sea, and he'd know in a heartbeat there's magic here – and poison, too.

The tide is low this morning. I slide downhill, muddying the hem of my lace skirt. I trudge through the black sand, beyond The Tide Pools, making my way to Wulver Cove. My father doesn't want me to visit the sea caves, so he tries to scare me with violent tales about wulvers who stalk the shores, searching for souls to steal.

Despite my father's gruesome stories, I go to Wulver Cove as often as I can; I feel closer to my mother there. I imagine her rocking me to sleep in the sea caves like she did all those years ago when I was just a baby. Once I'm inside, I sing my heart out. I don't remember the sound of my mother's voice, but the wind does, and if it blows just right, I hear her singing back to me, her voice breaking against the shell of my ear.

I kick off my boots and socks, warming my feet in the steamy water. As I listen to the gulls crying outside, my thoughts drift to poor Abilene. She's been with my family since The Mooring. I can't fathom how much she misses the sea. The landies wouldn't understand what we're doing, so we keep her hidden in The Hutch underground. Most of the time, I forget she's there, but when she cries at night, I feel sick with guilt.

To my family, Abilene is just a sea hag, but I know her true name. She told me so last month as she bathed in The Tide Pools. She also told me that Wulver Cove used to be a miraculous place. I want to believe it's true, but I suppose my family doesn't need miracles anymore, or castles, for that matter. We don't need moats or towers or gargoyle knockers. My father and uncle are living, breathing gargoyles, and none of the landies would ever dare cross them.

Even worse than my father and my uncle is the nasty brownie who guards the hawthorn tree behind our Blackhouse. He's not the friendly kind from candletime stories. He doesn't deal in sweeping and laundry. He deals in ghost ropes, blubber forks, and agony.

The brownie hates the drizzling rain, but I fancy every form of water. I love wet sand and sea spray and the stab of ice. I love the sapphire tide pools and the plunge of waterfalls down the sea cliffs. I love being battered by the waves on stormy days and the cold dip of the seafloor when my feet fly out from under me.

I rub my salty braid, stiff as a rope between my fingers. I pull my feet from the water and dry them with my wool cape. Then I slide into my socks and boots and climb the slippery cliffs before the damp settles in my bones. As I reach the top and round the corner, a petrel flutters through a piece of driftwood. Distracted, my foot slips out from under me, sending me backwards. I claw at the earth, pulling myself onto solid ground.

*Click. Click.* A pony whinnies in the distance.

I bet it's Clootie and the Constable paying us a visit. Diarmid visits us every month to check on my aunt Lorna. He's the only man foolish enough to poke his nose in our Blackhouse. I rock back on my heels and dash back home.

By the time I get there, Diarmid is already at the front door. I flash a sweet smile, though my mouth tastes like metal. Whenever he visits, I feel like retching. Lorna lives to torture him, and the sight of it makes me ill.

Lorna swings the door open, looking like a cat with a mouse. Diarmid stares as she sweeps up her butter-blonde hair, pinning it into a bun. His eyes linger there for a moment before dipping lower to the ruby locket crushed between her breasts.

I soak my hands in the wash basin, rolling my eyes.

Lorna holds up a hand, waving Diarmid into the kitchen. I trail behind them, drying my hands on my sleeves. It's gloomy inside, the walls deathly grey and scarred with ashes. The room swallows us in smoke and Diarmid coughs, trying to clear his throat.

I join my mother at the table, rubbing the hazy itch from my eyes. I help her roll the dough into balls of delight. I press them to my nose, welcoming the cloying scent of cinnamon and sugar.

Diarmid slumps down in the vacant chair near the hearth, swatting away a tendril of smoke.

"Don't sit there! That's the brownie's chair!" Lorna scolds him.

It's true. The brownie does sit there. I learned that the hard way when I was a little girl.

Mischievously, I sat down and pulled my knees to my chest, wearing nothing but a smile. I wanted to see if the brownie would show himself to me. Of course, he never did, but my father swore he was there.

Lovesick and half-afraid, Diarmid stands and stretches, then pokes at the fire. He looks even thinner than he did last month, his hip bones jutting out. Diarmid flicks his eyes at me, but I pretend not to see. Instead, I count the holes in his breeks. He glances over at Kilda's altar, with its wreath of rowan branches, lamb bones, and candle nubs, white wax stark against ashes. Diarmid tries to wear a brave mask, but his twitching beard gives him away.

Diarmid squares his shoulders and firms his lips, preparing to give a speech I've heard many times before. "After all these years, I deserve the truth, Lorna. It's no secret the bluebeards are from The Minch. You know as well as I do that nothing good ever comes from The Minch, just a bunch of wicked storm kelpies." Diarmid paces the floor, working himself up, as he always does. "It was Gunn who turned you against me, wasn't it? What kind of spell are you under?"

Lorna looks down her nose at him. "Must we have this conversation every time you visit? Honestly, Diarmid, it's so unseemly. How many times do I have to tell you? I'm not under a spell."

"That's the danger with spells. You could be under one and not know it."

"I'm the same person I was when we were together all those years ago. You just don't want to see it."

"That's not true, and I can prove it to you." Diarmid readies himself for the solution. I know what's coming before he says it. "If you leave Wulver Cove with me, the spell will break, and you'll remember what we had together." He pauses, his voice softening. "I know I'm not a strapping young lad anymore, but I've still got some life left in these bones. We can even take your sister and Senga with us."

Lorna gives him the cold shoulder, soaking her necessaries in a bucket of hot water. The air smells of lust and lavender. "Come now, darling. Who'd protect the landies if you left Hourglass Isle? Surely they'd perish without your grand dirk."

Diarmid raises an eyebrow. "There was a time when you loved my grand dirk."

Lorna smirks, inching closer to him. "Naturally. I had nothing else to compare it to."

He brushes a wisp of her hair from her cheek "And now that you do?"

"Truth be told –" she tortures him with a whispery breath, "– yours hit the mark."

Diarmid stands a little taller, his eyes gleaming.

Suddenly, the room is stuffy. I feel damp in soft places, my cheeks flushing. I know I shouldn't be privy to such conversations, but I can't pull myself away from their saga.

"Come away with me, my love," Diarmid coaxes. "We can leave tomorrow at dawn."

"And how would we get there? You don't have a feather to fly with. You're as poor as they come."

His eyes go dark. "And why do you think that is? Because Gunn stole everything from me, just like he stole everything from your father. Worst of all, you helped him do it."

Lorna raises her voice, hands on her hips. "You're so smug it sickens me. You're no better than Gunn. Your ancestors were raiders from The Stark Sea. You're as much a thief as Gunn is. Besides, this isle doesn't belong to anyone but Kilda."

"All the more reason to leave and find a place of our own. We're surrounded by uninhabited isles. We could build a new life together."

Lorna raises a mocking brow. "You mean you'd really abandon your haggard wife and your ragamuffins for me?"

Diarmid swallows his pride, his jaw tightening. "You know I would. When you came to the shipyard all those years ago and asked me to stay here, I gave up my father and my brothers for you, didn't I? You saw the tears in my eyes as we watched them sail back to The Stark Sea. Then you turned around and betrayed me, not to mention your father and your sister. How could you stand by and let Gunn destroy your family?" Diarmid is incensed now; I feel the heat of his fury. I hold my breath, expecting the worst. "Lord Goldie was a good man. Your father loved us, Lorna, and he wanted us to be happy. Don't you ever think of him?"

Lorna sulks, digging her heels into her boots, though she'll never admit to a wrong. "Some memories are better left buried. He's with my mother now, where he's always wanted to be. I'm sure he's much happier dead than he ever could've been alive, so no harm was done."

"Surely you don't believe that," Diarmid says incredulously. "Your father is dead. The castle is a pile of ashes. The landies are starving. And if none of those things matter to you, then just look at your sister. She hasn't spoken in years. And you say there's no spell here. Well, I don't believe you!" Diarmid's ink-blue eyes threaten to spill.

Lorna cuts him to ribbons with her sharp tongue. "You're insufferable, Diarmid. You're the one who chases after me when you have a house full of shrieking children. Have you ever asked your family what they've had to sacrifice because you won't let me go? And while we're on the subject, why must your children cry and pout so much? It's pathetic."

His cheeks flush mauve. "All children cry. It's natural."

"It's far from natural. Why, our dear Senga was good as gold. She never pouted or wailed. She only cried when it was necessary, and when she did, it was ever so softly." Lorna pauses, leaning in for the kill. “Children take after their fathers. The bluebeards are strong, and you’re weak.”

Diarmid scowls, clenching the dirk on his hip. “Strong? Is that what you call it? Gunn isn’t strong. He’s a monster. Is that what you want me to be? A monster? Would you love me then? Just say the words, and I’ll cobble myself into the scariest monster you’ve ever seen.”

“Come now, darling, be reasonable,” Lorna says silkily. “You could never be a monster. Why must you come here and torture yourself every month? You should go home to your family. How many times do I have to tell you? I don’t love you anymore. As far as I can tell, the only fool under a spell is *you*.”

Diarmid falters for a moment, his legs soft as jelly. “There’s no need to throw daggers at each other.”

Lorna smirks. “Believe me, darling, if I threw a dagger at you, you wouldn’t be standing.”

He squares his shoulders, refusing to surrender. “Don’t you remember those cold nights in The Brittle Forest together? Squeezing through The Wee Narrows, chasing goblins, kissing each other by firelight? We were so happy. Please, tell me you remember.” He reaches out to touch the ruby locket around her neck.

Lorna rears back. “Of course I remember, but I’m not a sentimental fool like you are. Why must you live in a house of misery?”

"You're the one who trapped me there when you begged me to stay all those years ago!" Diarmid snaps. "How could you forsake me, Lorna? How could you forsake your family and the landies who loved you? If the bluebeards didn't cast a spell on you, then perhaps it was Kilda."

"Kilda has done nothing to me that I didn't want her to do. I'm not her victim."

"Kilda be damned if she's cursed you."

Lorna turns up her nose, her lips drawn thin. "Only a fool would damn a god. You truly are a maddening creature. The sooner you realize I'm not the helpless maiden you think I am, the better off we'll both be. If there's a damsel milling about on this isle, it's not me." Lorna flashes an icepick of a smile. "Perhaps it's you, darling. Perhaps you're the damsel in the tower."

He grits his teeth. "I'm no more a damsel than you are a lady."

Lorna's eyes glimmer, more amused than insulted. "Well, you could've fooled me with all your hysterics. I've never heard a man whine as much as you do."

"Why are you so petulant, Lorna? What have I ever done to deserve your heart of stone?"

I'm ashamed of myself for witnessing Diarmid's humiliation. I should've excused myself long ago. I glance over at my mother for help, but I can't glean anything from her. She carries on as if nothing has happened, stuffing the soul cakes with walnuts and pumpkin.

Diarmid follows my gaze to my mother. “How are you, Twila, old friend?”

She gives him a cursory nod, her lips oyster-tight, then she goes back to dusting the soul cakes with cinnamon.

When Lorna turns away, my mother snags a sweetmeat from a silver tray and slips it to Diarmid. I suspect she feels sorry for him, the poor, eel-thin man with a broken heart. I feel sorry for him, too. There’s something rather sad about the plaid vest under his cloak, such merry colors for a shriveling body.

“Twila, please, help me. There’s got to be a hutch or a trapdoor around here somewhere,” Diarmid pleads.

My mother gurgles, but no words come out. She wipes the drool from her lips, then tucks a loose curl behind her ear.

“I know you didn’t want to marry Warr. I know your heart belonged to another. I can bring the bluebeards to justice if you show me where The Hutch is.” In a violent thump, Diarmid drops to his knees and worms his way across the floor. He pounds his fists into the grit, searching for a trapdoor. “It’s such a shame about your mother,” Diarmid laments, glancing up at me. “If only you could’ve heard her sing. She had the voice of a nightingale.”

The air sharpens, each breath a stab to my lungs. I’ve heard the landies gossiping about my mother and father before but hearing it from Diarmid makes it all the more real. I feel a prickle on the nape of my neck. A moment later, my father and Gunn charge into the kitchen.

Gunn glowers at Diarmid, pulling his dirk from its sheath. "Whatever you're searching for, you won't find it here. You better think long and hard before you come into my blackhouse again. Next time, I just might rip your insides out."

My father snorts, kicking Diarmid in the belly, knocking the wind out of him. I know how bad it hurts because my father has kicked me with his hoof-feet many times. In a daze, Diarmid stumbles to the door and scrambles outside. He hurries to his pony without looking back.

After the ruckus is over, we sit down for supper. The oak table is so long and wide, and the chairs so far apart, that we can't really carry on a conversation, but it doesn't bother me in the slightest. I don't want to talk to them, anyway.

The brownie reclines in the vacant chair at the head of the table, his bowl full of honeycomb brittle. I can't see him, but I know he's there. Lorna coils like a serpent, her eyes glowing. My mother offers my grandmother's ghost a soul cake. My father slurps on lamb and bean stew while Gunn guzzles mead from his silver horn. I force myself to swallow the last spoonful of my meal so I can go to bed.

Half past candletime, I'm still awake, with Diarmid's words racing through my head.

*It's no secret the bluebeards are from The Minch. You know as well as I do that nothing good ever comes from The Minch, just a bunch of wicked storm kelpies.*

# 5

## The Mermaid Chorus

Kilda has everything she's ever wanted. She wears a crown of berries and antlers, and the fallows worship her in smoke and shadows, but such spoils are not enough. The Brittle Forest is not what she dreamed, and neither are the fallows. Kilda longs to return to the sea, to feel the slip of fins and the rush of water. With a lonesome whistle, she strokes the hollow notch where her heart used to beat, her roots pinning her to the ground.

Rain pours from the bleak sky, slicking her branches with ice, but Kilda clings to a glimmer of hope. The bluebeards of The Minch are finally awake and sailing towards Hourglass Isle. Their vessel pierces the gloom, its black sails flapping in the wind.

Of all the eternals, the bluebeards are the most vulnerable to Kilda's dark little magic, for they were fast asleep during The Great Divide, and they know nothing of her betrayal. Kilda knows she must act fast if she's to make a covenant with them. If she can persuade them to slay the queenfish and steal the cup of immortality, then she can finally return to the sea. Kilda shivers in anticipation, waiting for the bluebeards, when an unfortunate fallow disturbs her.

"May I beg a moment of your time, Your Majesty?"

Kilda snatches him by his antlers and spears him with her branches.

He thrashes in her sap-sticky arms. “Please forgive my blunder,” he gurgles, drowning in blood.

“I don’t have time for foolish questions,” Kilda seethes, smashing him against the sea cliffs. With a wrinkled smile, she pokes his antlers into her crown and licks the gore from her fingers.

“Let that be a lesson to you all. I’m in no mood.” She considers tormenting the other fallows, but the thunder of drums steals her attention and a shanty echoes in the wind.

*Heave away, heave away.*
*Away we all roll, bound for The Bitter Sea.*
*Where women are warm, and glory is nigh, and blood-red is the sky.*
*Where bellies are full, and boots are dry.*
*Tully o’, tully o’, rum, rum, rye.*
*Heave away, heave away.*
*Away we all roll, bound for The Bitter Sea.*
*The waves be our wings is the song that we sing.*
*To The Bitter Sea we fly.*

Kilda rattles with anticipation, sap dripping from her fingers. She stretches her roots as far as she can and bends her trunk towards the sea. A petrel with a broken wing tumbles from one of her branches.

The bluebeards gather on the quarterdeck, rubbing their eyes in disbelief.

“I have a riddle for you,” Kilda lures, her wrinkled trunk mounting the waves.

The bluebeards lean over the starboard, shocked at such a sight.

“When a man meets a god, what should he do?”

Tongue-tied, they dare not speak a word.

“Believe,” she commands. “I am Kilda, the god of Hourglass Isle. And while you slumbered underwater for centuries, I held the weight of the land on my shoulders. Long ago, you were glorious storm kelpies, but you’ve slept away your power. Just look at your slack bellies and mangy beards. You’re nothing without me,” she lies, her lips a spatter of leaves.

Strangely aroused, they stare at her grassy hair and knobby breasts.

“I’m willing to make you an offer. If you do my bidding, I’ll give you fair maidens to ravish, fine ponies to ride, unsinkable luggers, and all the glory your hearts desire. Are there any hungry souls among you?”

Intrigued, a pair of grubby brothers cry out to her. “We’re hungry souls. What would you have us do?”

“For every child you have, you must capture one mermaid during The Mooring each summer and slay her on The Feast of the Singing Wound the following autumn. If you do this for me, I’ll give you riches and glory. But I’ll give you even more if you catch the queenfish.”

“What does she look like?” the eldest brother asks, aiming his spit overboard.

“I can’t tell you, but if you catch her, I’ll turn you into gods, and we’ll rule Hourglass Isle together.”

The brothers fall to their knees and bow their heads.

Kilda swims closer to them, muddling their minds with her dark little magic. “You must bind yourself to me and satisfy my hunger. Do you swear to do my bidding and teach your families the same, no matter how wicked?”

“Yes, Your Majesty. We pledge ourselves and our families to you.”

“Will you take me as your god and live under my dark little magic as humans?”

“Yes, Your Majesty,” they vow, kissing her gnarled branches.

“Then you must capture Wulver Cove and besiege Goldie Castle. It’ll be a bloody battle, but I’ll make it worth your effort. Two fair maidens wait for you with hair of spindled gold and lips red as roses. Tarry not. To the victor goes the spoils.” With a shrill whistle, Kilda springs from the waves and ascends the sea cliffs. Water turns to wood, and she disappears into The Brittle Forest.

# 6

## Senga

Raindrops spill through the cracked roof, anointing my head with sorrow. I swear my father and Gunn summon a squall every time Diarmid visits. But I'm letting it all go, if only for a moment, surfing the waves of sleep. Everything is warm and fuzzy until thunder claps above me.

An image of Diarmid swims through my vision, and my blood runs cold. My heart aches just thinking about him. He'll never find The Hutch because he's looking in all the wrong places. I know, because I've looked in the same places. My father is a sleekit devil. He knows better than to keep a hutch inside The Blackhouse. Though I play dumb when Diarmid visits, I know exactly where The Hutch is hidden. It's under the hawthorn tree behind The Blackhouse, and the nasty brownie guards it.

I roll over, fighting the current of nightmares that threaten to pull me under: the waterspout spinning around me, the needle and thread goring my legs, the blubber fork glittering against my throat, harp strings whipping in the wind.

In the half-light of dawn, the brownie stalks me. I see him so clearly. A cinder-elf with flames for fingers, eyes black as coal, long, candlestick teeth, and cobwebbed hair. He grins at me, flicking his serpent tongue. One lick of his venom, and I'd be dead.

Frantically, I rouse myself awake. I jump out of bed and pace the dirt floor. Does the brownie know my secrets? Does he spy on me through the cracked roof? Does he know who I think about when I touch my tender parts under the sheets? I grab the rock I keep under my bed. If the brownie ever shows himself to me, I'll smash his skull in with it.

But the brownie isn't the only one I'm angry at. I'm also angry at Gunn and my father. Gunn says the most disgusting things to me, and my father does nothing to stop him.

*Now, that you've bled, beware the brownie. If you don't behave, he'll crawl into your bed while you sleep and lick the honeypot between your legs. And he'll give you warts and a wee bundle in your belly*

I want to scream at the top of my lungs. Gunn has no right to talk about my honeypot. He shouldn't even *think* about my honeypot. My father should defend my honor and break every bone in Gunn's body.

I wish my grandfather was still alive. He'd protect me, and he'd never talk to me that way or spy on me. I long to know what happened to him and his castle, but perhaps it's better I don't know. The truth might crush me.

# 7

# The Mermaid Chorus

There once was a lord who lived in a castle perched on a windswept bluff, high above the salt. Lord Goldie had two daughters with hair of spindled gold and lips as red as roses. A rather peculiar lord, he was loved by all the landies on Hourglass Isle. Though many shadows had darkened him, his heart wasn't bitter. Lord Goldie turned every last cinder into shine; even his name was golden.

There was a place for everyone in Lord Goldie's castle, and he shared his riches with the landies. He took in drifters, offering them room and board in exchange for simple chores: harvesting herbs, peeling potatoes, mending clothes, sharpening arrows. He even dined with the wulvers, who tried to warn him of Kilda's dark little magic.

Although Lord Goldie was deeply loved, he pined for his wife, Rowena, who had died giving birth to their youngest daughter, Lorna. Lord Goldie buried his wife's body below the salt, but she couldn't bear to leave her husband and her daughters, so her spirit took shelter in the castle's turret. For many moons, her ghost lingered with them, and they were a happy family.

Every morning, Twila and Lorna woke to their mother's sweet voice trilling like a dove in the clouds. They followed her melody, racing each other up the tower. Inside the turret, they danced with her ghost and baked her soul cakes on her birthday.

They shared many merry seasons together until tragedy struck their family again. When Twila and Lorna were of age to marry, the bluebeards besieged Goldie Castle. Hungry for power, Lorna gave her heart to Gunn. He was the grittiest man she'd ever known, willing to kill to get what he wanted, and Kilda's blessing was upon him.

Lorna tried to persuade Twila to marry Gunn's brother, Warr. But Twila refused, for she'd already given her heart to an eternal. With her father's blessing, she planned to make her escape at dawn the next morning. She dreaded leaving her father, but she knew it was only a matter of time before Warr forced himself on her.

On the eve of her escape, Twila slumped down in the chair beside the dressing table. She gazed into the gold-leaf mirror, her amber eyes flooding with tears. She stood with a sigh and swished over to the window, her heavy skirts fanning around her. Twila tugged on the burgundy drapes and peered into the darkness. She was tempted to flee the castle in the dark of night, but she knew she needed a splash of dawn's early light to guide her to Crescent Isle.

Twila searched for comfort. She took up her mother's harp and plucked it with her slender fingers, and when she sang, her voice vibrated like an angel. It was her way of saying goodbye, for it was the last night she'd ever spend in the castle.

Twila drew a shallow breath and laid the harp to rest. She padded over to the emerald settee, soft enough for fainting. She loosened her corset and reclined by the crackling fire. She shut her weary eyes, but sleep eluded her.

At the pink of dawn, Twila crept out of the castle. She sidled through the rose garden, inhaling the wintry perfume of frosted petals. With frayed nerves, she looked over her shoulder, taking great pains to ensure she wasn't being followed.

Twila carefully descended the sea cliffs, hugging the narrow trail, until she reached the black sand. She skittered between The Tide Pools, slogging her way to the shore. The fog was thick as mud, but she knew the path well, and she trusted her father's plan. Just then, Twila caught a glimpse of her father at the water's edge, kneeling beside a crude raft. She ran to him and buried her face in his chest.

Lord Goldie kissed her forehead, his damp eyes shining like wet stones. "It's not much, but it'll get to you Crescent Isle. I built it with my own hands."

"I can't leave you, father. Please, come with me. We can escape together," she cried.

"Not without your sister. I must do everything I can to save Lorna. Don't fret over me. I'll be just fine."

Twila sighed, casting him a weary glance.

"Your true love is waiting for you on Crescent Isle. You mustn't tarry any longer," her father urged, helping her into the raft.

There was a great splash as her father pushed her out to sea. Tears streamed down Twila's cheeks, a mingle of joy and sorrow, but her sorrow was far from over.

Moments later, Warr sprang from the sea with the rising sun. "You *will* be my wife, whether you like it or not," he shouted, his beard frothing with the waves. In one fell swoop, Warr seized the raft and hauled Twila back to the castle while Gunn wrestled with Lord Goldie on the black sand.

Back inside, where the walls glittered, Lorna scolded her sister. "I know you can't see it now, but this marriage is for your own good. Warr is the right man for you. He –"

Gunn interrupted Lorna with a growl. "What should we do with your father? He tried to help Twila escape. He must be punished."

"Shackle him and take him to the dungeon," Lorna ordered. "Twila is just as guilty, if not more, but I'll spare her the chains if she agrees to marry Warr."

Warr grinned.

"But you know I've already given my heart to another!" Twila cried.

Lorna twirled a strand of hair around her finger. "Promises are fragile and easily broken. I'm the lady of the castle now, and you'll obey my orders."

Lord Goldie turned white as a sail. "But Twila is the rightful heir of the castle!"

"Heavy is the head that wears the crown," Lorna said with a smile. "I'd hate to see her pretty neck snap under its weight."

Lord Goldie shuddered at the thought. "What have you done, Lorna? You've called on Kilda, haven't you?"

Lorna turned up her nose and sneered. "Oh, father, you sound just like Diarmid. You always were a foolish man, inviting wulvers and drifters to dine at our table when you should've been inviting men like Gunn and Warr."

Within the hour, Lord Goldie was thrown into the dungeon, and the next evening at sunset, the Goldie sisters married the bluebeard brothers. Their union made Kilda's dark little magic even stronger. Poison latched onto the land like barnacles. The days were long, the years even longer. Twila was tempted to throw herself into the sea, but she couldn't bear the thought of leaving her father.

On a windy summer morning, Twila awoke in a blanket of smoke. She sprung from bed and grabbed her mother's harp and tomes, then she shook her daughter awake, and they fled the castle.

Fiery chaos swirled around them. Her mother's urn cracked open, new flames eating old ashes. Twila draped her robe over her daughter, trying to shield her from the smoke. The little girl stumbled alongside her mother, fear creeping through her bones. Staircases crumbled and portraits bled through frames, erasing years of legacy. Mirrors melted, painting the walls a furious gold.

They staggered outside and fell to their knees, their lungs burning with smoke. Twila looked around, observing her surroundings. Though her daughter was rattled, she was still alive, coughing and rubbing the ashes from her eyes.

But something was terribly wrong.

"Father! Where's father? Did anyone bring him up from the dungeon? We must save him!" Twila screamed, sobbing in the charred grass.

But it was too late, for Lord Goldie had perished in the flames.

# 8

## Diarmid

The Teahouse is full of ghosts. For all I know, I'm one of them. An anchor that will never leave this isle. A casualty of Kilda's poison. Lorna says I'm the one under a spell. *Dark little magic*, she calls it. Even if I am under a spell, is it any wonder? Man or ghost can't think straight when he's starving.

I scope out the room, taking note of each soul. Smoke curls through loose teeth. Bones crunch on stiff chairs. Brittle hair splits over skulls. We, the landies, are stark raving hungry, but we don't come to The Teahouse to eat. We come here to dream.

Sir Craig pats me on the back. "What's your pleasure, Constable?"

"Sausage pie, tattie cakes, fried tomatoes, scones, and marmalade."

"Your wish is my command." He smiles at me, his mouth a shipwreck of teeth, then he scurries off into the kitchen.

While I dream of a feast piled high, a gale batters The Teahouse. I pull my cloak tighter, fending off the chill as rain leaks through the windows. A minute later, Sir Craig hands me a dry biscuit and a mug of watery coffee. Munching on stale crumbs, I can almost taste the tang of marmalade on my tongue. It reminds me of Lorna, sweet and tart. It's been too long since I've tasted her lips and thighs and everything in between.

The Teahouse turns me on, but I'm not the only one. It's a bedrock of pleasure, tempting the landies with smutty red lanterns and sweet cherry brandy, and Lady Graham wouldn't have it any other way. She's always had a penchant for intimate delights, and she loves playing matchmaker for landies and drifters alike.

I glance over my shoulder, eyeing her latest match. Bareback Bonnie is pinned against the wall as a man's head swims through her underskirts. She slides to the floor, begging for more, urging him on with a muffled scream. Conversations swirl about, tongues licking and men dreaming of juicy thighs and tea cakes slathered in butter.

A thrill pulses through me, my anatomy thoroughly engaged. I take a sip of coffee, turning my attention to a drifter. He sits at a corner table, with briny eyes and a white-capped beard, his hands scarred with rope burns. After last night's romp, I bet he's ready to shove off and return to the sea. I wonder who pleased him behind the flimsy curtain in the dark of night? Perhaps the widow Lusk or bareback Bonnie? No, neither of them. A smile tugs on my lips. I bet a dram of whiskey it was little Aila. Between her webbed feet and his peg leg, what a sight *that* would be. I choke on a peal of laughter.

The drifter locks eyes with me; perhaps he knows what I'm thinking. I straighten my spine, nodding politely. He swigs the last drop in his mug, then wobbles to his feet. Favoring his good leg, he pushes through the front door and onward to the brackish sea.

Seized by an impulse, I dash to the window. Outside, a crowd of men are boarding an ironclad vessel. It doesn't take me long to spot the peg-legged drifter. I want to go wherever he's going, and I want to take Lorna with me. Time is but a waning candle. Before long, I'll be dying on the dark edges, the wick of my life spent and sputtering. I stare at the bleak horizon, watching the drifter sail away until he's nothing but a speck of sea glass in the wind.

I have more in common with these drifters than they realize, and I owe it all to my brave father who sailed The Stark Sea. Most of the time, I try not to think about my father. I prefer to keep him locked away in the secret chamber of my heart, but today he haunts me, along with all the other ghosts in the teahouse.

My father takes the shape of a shadow, drifting closer to me. He raises a mug to our motherland, his whale of a voice clicking in my ears.

*Sail north with us, my boy. Come and meet your ancestors. There's a place for you in the whitewashed mountains. There's peace in the icefields. Lorna will only forsake you, and the bluebeards will destroy this isle. Save yourself before it's too late.*

I should've sailed north with my father. The grief burns in my belly, even stronger than my hunger. Why did I stay on this damned isle?

Behind closed eyes, I drift back in time, finding the answer to my question. I see Lorna running through The Brittle Forest, her moonlit hair ribboning in the wind. She's all that I can see; she's all that matters. Craving the flames of her fire, I chase until I catch her. With one caress, Lorna turns my aching body into a hearth. Lost in her berry-black eyes, I'm nothing but wood and embers, sparking in her arms.

Lorna sprawls out on the forest floor, bare-naked and smiling. She pulls me closer, kissing my lips, pressing the length of me inside her. I feel the sharp edge of my desire, but even when I'm slick with the nectar of her blossom, there's only love, pure and true, and I would smoke myself into a burnt offering if she asked me to.

As the memory subsides, I return to my lonely table, wine-stained and scarred with fork stabs. There's no greater agony than knowing the truth and not being able to prove it. I'm certain Kilda beguiled the Goldie sisters into marrying the bluebeards. There's no other explanation but a sinister spell cast by a petulant god.

Now, nothing is the way it should be. I'm sick of living in a house of misery. I should be with Lorna. Twila should be with her true love, and Ivor should be with Senga.

# 9

## Senga

It's no secret I fancy Ivor. How could I not? He refuses to bend his knee for Kilda, and he's the only man brave enough to fish in my father's waters. Ivor is something of a legend on Hourglass Isle. Rumor has it he descended from the wulvers who worshipped the moon and the stars.

Ivor lost his family a long time ago. Some say they drowned in a terrible storm. Others say they were murdered, their spirits haunting the sea caves, seeking revenge on those who destroyed them. I wish I could ask Ivor what really happened, but I don't want him to think I'm a nosy mouse. We all have secrets buried in our hearts.

Ivor is my secret; the dream I touch under the sheets when the candles sputter out.

At night, I imagine Ivor slipping through the cracked roof in my room. My body rises to meet him, and we float in the smoking dark above my bed. All shivers and whispers, I stroke the rough of his jaw. He wastes no time in ravishing me. He crushes my waist in his hands, thrusting his length inside me. In the afterglow, Ivor sings to the hollow notch inside me, where hope burned bright before I learned how wicked the world could be. Before I learned I could never marry Ivor.

I know Ivor is my elder, but he makes me tingle, the same feeling I get when I eat a raw oyster. He's nothing like the other men, sheet-pale and scrawny. Ivor is a wall of rock I want to climb; a swirl of honey I want to lick; the most dapper man on Hourglass Isle. Granted, he has a dead eye, but when I gaze into it, I can predict the weather. I hear gales and thunder. I smell moss and rain. And when he smiles at me, I melt into a puddle.

In due time, the handful of years between us won't matter. Besides, there are men far worse than Ivor, like the bluebeards who think they own every pretty creature and the scamps with rotten teeth who beg me to sit on their knees.

My family doesn't make merry at The Teahouse on Hogmanay, but my mother sees to it that I'm in attendance. She wants me to clink mugs with the landies and be part of their community, even if it's only once a year. Had she not married my father, the landies would be my friends and Ivor would be my husband.

Last year on Hogmanay, before the festivities began, the landies bowed their heads and prayed to Kilda. They only did it to please me, because they thought I worshipped her like the rest of my family. I couldn't tell them any different, so I bowed my head, but Ivor saw through my false prayer. He brushed his lips against my ear, his voice a deep, dark whisper sending a flutter through my heart.

Ivor eased back in his chair, looking handsome as ever, his almond eyes glowing in the torchlight. He wore a black tunic over his broad shoulders and a cloak trimmed in salt and pepper fur. When he stood, his breeks clung to him in all the right places, leaving little to my imagination.

Ivor offered me his hand, helping me to my feet. Even on my tiptoes, he towered over me. My eyes landed on his neck, covered in ink. I traced my fingers along the hourglass etched on his skin. He rolled his shoulders back, looking more animal than human, his throat stirring with a needful sound. A shiver swam through me as I imagined the rough of his tongue between my thighs. I fought the urge to tear off his belt and search for hidden ink.

For a breath, I feared Ivor was a figment of my imagination. There was only one way to be sure, so I slid my palm over his forearm, my nails cutting deep, eating away at his flesh. He flinched, flashing me a fang-toothed smile. A pearl of blood glistened on his skin. He smeared it with his fingers while his dark eyes lingered on my breasts. A faint howl rose from his throat, a torturesome pleasure caught in his mouth.

*Howls and fangs*. Surely they were tricks of the torchlight, spawned by sweet cherry brandy and corsets pulled too tight. I tugged on the severe fabric, desperate to catch a shallow breath.

Ivor was on the verge of asking me to dance. I heard the words on the tip of his tongue. The moment was perfect – until Mina MacTavish arrived.

# 10

# Ivor

When a man fishes, he catches things lost long ago. His nets are never empty, always full. Full of memories, melding with scales and claws, blurring the line between then and now. A man never knows which memory he'll catch, but he must reel it in, good or bad, and welcome it with all his heart.

I am that man, welcoming a memory. Last December, under the cold moon. Hogmanay. Snow falling, soft and true.

Senga sits beside me, a white rose tucked behind her ear. Under the soft glow of torchlight, she's a sight to behold, all ridges and valleys, painted lips and cinched waist. Much to my delight, a plunging dress takes the place of her usual high-necked blouse. Black velvet clings to her in all the right places. The lace of her bodice bursts at the seams, her nipples nearly visible. Her scarlet hair hangs in a loose bun, perched like a bird on her shoulder. I drink her in, the smooth of her skin, the twist of her collarbone.

As lovely as Senga is, I won't dance with her this year, for the river of blood has washed her into a woman. I regret wounding her pride, but I must keep my distance. Not to mention, Mina MacTavish expects my hand in my marriage.

I stand from my chair, grating the wooden legs against the stone floor. Senga tilts her head, gazing up at me. Softly, I kiss her cheek and excuse myself from her presence. She bites back a frown, her lips pressed thin.

I try to make merry with the landies. We talk of poles and lines, nets and creels, but my heart's not in the conversation. My dead eye drifts towards Senga, the torchlight playing on her face. If she wasn't Warr's daughter, men would fight to the death just to dance with her.

Senga catches me staring at her. She bats her eyes and crinkles her nose. We have our own little language of unspoken words.

Two years ago, she told me a silent secret, her eyes a spill of sea glass, sharp-green and sad. *No one loves me.*

The next Hogmanay, I gave her a gift. It took several dives, but in time, I found a beautiful black pearl. Beneath the dimming candelabra, I crept behind Senga and hooked the rosette around her neck. She smiled over her shoulder, blushing down to the roots of her hair.

In the quiet dark, words rang through my heart, words I longed to say out loud. *I love you, Senga.*

Suddenly, Sir Craig elbows me, and the memory bleeds away. He studies me for a beat, his face pulled tight with salt and sun. "Are you still with us, Ivor? Tell us your trick for setting creels."

I feel my way through time, digging my heels into the present moment, only to find Mina flitting towards me, fussing with a cockeyed hat too big for her head. Mina greets Sir Craig with a cursory smile, lest she look ill-mannered, but we all know her intention is to persuade me. Sir Craig offers her a friendly nod, then takes his leave.

"The evening is half-spent, turtledove. Shall we dance?" Mina buzzes around me like a fly I want to swat away, but I can't refuse her, not after what her father did for me.

Mina is an old maid, a hundred and seventy moons older than me. When I was a boy, she washed my breeks, stitched my knees, and told me candletime stories. She's more like a mother to me than anything else. But I have a debt to repay, and she knows it.

"What do you say?" Mina whispers with moldy breath.

I swallow hard, trying not to bristle. "Of course."

Mina clutches my shoulders, her breasts falling flat against my chest. Her dress swims around her, billowing like a sail. Mina huffs with irritation as I search for her waist. She pulls me closer, poking me with her worn-out springs. Finally, I snag her hip bones and she whimpers with delight. Mina is in my arms now, but I'm leagues away, my dead eye searching for Senga.

Moments later, I find her whispering with Lady Graham. It's a sight to see them standing next to each other: Senga, with high cheekbones and lips dark as hellebore, and Lady Graham, tree-tall and rough as sandpaper, her greasy hair slicked behind her ears.

After a frightful bout of wheezing, Lady Graham returns to smoking her pipe. She sweeps her grey eyes across the room, searching for someone, *anyone,* to pair with Senga. There's nothing Lady Graham loves more than playing matchmaker. She breaks into a grin, waving at a handsome stranger. I've never seen him before; perhaps he's a drifter.

Senga glances at me, burying the black pearl in the hollow of her throat. She shimmers like a cold moon in a velvet sky, and I catch the chill in her bones. How badly I want to sink my teeth into her pale neck and draw blood as red as her hair.

Then it happens: the worst thing I can imagine. A boy on the verge of a man takes Senga by the hand, and she follows him into the snug. I beg the stars he doesn't touch her, or even worse, kiss her. I swallow the lump in my throat, conjuring a merry memory.

Like the day Senga was born.

All through that night, the copper bells rang in her honor. Senga was my betrothed. Her mother told me so. I didn't know what it meant at the time, only that it made me happy. Our love was etched in stone, and nothing else mattered.

# 11

## Diarmid

While Sorcha sleeps in our bed, I sulk at the table with an empty belly. I hardly sleep anymore; my head barely makes a dent in the pillow. If I was a braver man, I'd ride to Lorna's blackhouse and slay the bluebeards with my bare hands. I'd feast on milk, lamb, scones, and jam. I'd have Lorna in bed, begging for more, gasping with pleasure. But I'm not that kind of man, much to my dismay.

I've tried so hard to bond with Sorcha and my children. I want to be a man worthy of their affection, but I've made too many errors along the way. I've spent so much time chasing after Lorna that I've lost sight of what's right in front of me. I glance over at my son, fast asleep on a pillow of pine needles by the hearth. Every season, his cough gets worse, and his fever weakens him.

But insight is no match for emotion. Not even my son can curb my appetite for Lorna. I'm a hungry man and she's bait on the line. A memory hooks me, dragging me back to last November.

I'm sitting in The Teahouse, dreaming of Lorna. The tea bell chimes and a familiar face appears. It's Ivor, the legend, in flesh and blood. He's not even twenty years old yet, and already he's a rock of a man.

The landies leap for joy, eager to buy him a dram of whiskey. I can't help but notice they've never bought me a dram of anything, and I'm the Constable of this isle, but I can't succumb to jealousy. Ivor is a good friend to me and worthy of my blessing.

After Kilda struck our cattle with milk fever, we turned to fishing for sustenance. It should be easy to catch fish on an isle, but it's not. I've tried fishing from every vantage point I can fathom, but even the fish are beguiled by Kilda. I've seen it with my own eyes. They swim to the shallows of Wulver Cove, right into the bluebeards' nets.

I drum my fingers on the table, considering the cold, hard facts. Ivor is the only man brave enough to cast his net near Wulver Cove and the only man lucky enough to catch anything. On happy mornings, I find a basket of hake and herring on my doorstep. If it weren't for Ivor, I'd have to beg the bluebeards just to feed my children. In light of the misery Ivor has spared me, I leap to my feet, cheering him on.

"Did you catch anything today?" Lady Graham asks, lighting her pipe.

Ivor flashes a smile. "Your bellies will be full tonight."

Lady Graham thumps him on the back. "You've done it again, Ivor. You've bought us more time in this world, though I don't know why any of us would want it," she says drolly.

Sir Craig raises his mug. "Hear, hear!"

Ivor drapes an arm around me and I feel his imposing height. He angles us away from the landies. "I found something you'll want to see, Constable."

"What did you find?"

"Let's talk outside."

We slip out the front door into the drizzling rain. I swallow the lump in my throat, begging the question again. "What did you find, Ivor?"

"A body washed ashore, and she's in bad shape."

"Is it Lorna? Please tell me it's not Lorna," I cry.

"Of course not. I would've told you right away if it was," Ivor bites, gritting his teeth.

I breathe a sigh of relief. "It may not be Lorna today, but it could be tomorrow. The bluebeards are savage beasts. You know it as well as I do. I have no doubt they're responsible for the body you found. I've tried to warn Lorna about them, but she won't listen to me."

Ivor rubs his weathered hands together, his nostrils flaring. "I know better than anyone how wicked the bluebeards are, but we need to consider other possibilities. For all we know, there could be another predator loose on our isle. I think you should examine the body before making accusations."

"You're right," I yield, rubbing my rain-slick beard. "Did you recognize the body? Was she a landie?"

Ivor swallows hard. "I don't think so. I don't even know if she's human."

"Of course she's human. What else could she be?"

"I can't quite put my finger on it, but there was something so peculiar about her," Ivor says, his eerie tone leaving me unsettled.

My skin crawls with memories of bloody torsos and severed tongues. "She's not the first body to wash ashore," I say, furrowing my brow.

"You mean this has happened before? Why didn't you tell me?"

"There have been other bodies over the years, but you were just a boy. It wouldn't have been right to expose you to such gore." As we slog to the pony pen, I tighten my cloak against the bitter wind. "I'd be much obliged if you'd lead me to the body since it's on the way to your croft."

"Of course. We should make haste before nightfall." Ivor strides ahead of me, mounting his pony with ease. Ivor and Broon are the perfect pair, all chestnut eyes and sleek muscles.

I'm not nearly as graceful or as handsome. Clootie looks up at me, his shabby eyes full of sorrow. I pat his blond rump, before making a rather awkward mount. I squirm for a good minute, straightening myself out. Clootie lets out a snort, following Broon into the gloom.

All is quiet until I hear Ivor's voice on the wind. "The body isn't far from Gunn and Lorna's blackhouse."

"You mean *Lorna's* blackhouse," I say curtly. "Gunn thinks he owns everything on this damned isle, but he doesn't. A thief can't own anything, now, can he?"

Ivor glares at me over his shoulder, pinning me with his gaze. "Believe me, Diarmid, I despise the bluebeards even more than you do. All you ever seem to care about is what they did to Lorna. Surely you haven't forgotten what they did to my family."

I look away, my mouth dry as cotton. "I'm sorry, Ivor. I know you've lost more than I could ever imagine. Kilda's dark little magic has ruined our isle."

Ivor rolls his eyes, tamping down his irritation. "You give Kilda too much power. She's not as strong as you think. Aren't you tired of feeling angry and bitter? Don't you want to believe in something greater than Kilda?"

"What greater power is there than Kilda? If you need proof of Kilda's dominion, just look at what she did to Twila. The poor woman hasn't spoken in years. And Lorna would've never married a bluebeard if it weren't for Kilda's dark little magic."

"Perhaps Lorna and Twila made their own decisions. As for me, I believe in something older and truer than Kilda. Can't you feel it all around you? The land is soaked in blood and tears – not of Kilda, but of your family and mine."

*My family*. A knot swells in my belly. The earth churns like a cold river. Rain clouds spill from the sky, splattering the trail into a muddy mess. Winter is just around the corner. I can already smell the brine of seabirds on their nests.

When we reach the dreaded spot, Broon halts abruptly. Ivor casts me a stormy look, his eyes full of thunder.

Hastily, I leap from Clootie, flailing through the air. I try to untangle my legs but to no avail. I land on my knees. Pain cracks through me, dizzying me on the spot.

Ivor dismounts Broon and helps me to my feet. "Are you alright?"

"I am, but my pride's not," I grumble.

"The body isn't far from here, just west of the rocky outcrop. Do you want me to come with you?" Ivor asks, his face paling.

"You've already seen the ghastly sight once today. I won't subject you to it again. Just keep an eye on Clootie. I'll be back soon."

An angry wind whistles through the driftwood. I light a candle, quickly covering it with a glass chimney. I stumble through shades of grey and skitter over bleached rocks.

On the fringes of light, I see *her*: a cloven body dipped in blood.

Stalking forward, I close the gap between us. Her cinnamon hair burns through the fog, twining around her like seaweed. A jade pendant plunges between her breasts while her nipples play hide-and-seek under a pair of starfish. I'm tempted to peek underneath. What color would her nipples be? Blackberry or peaches and cream?

A thrill pulses through me, hardening my anatomy. For a shameful moment, all reason abandons me. It wouldn't take much to satisfy my need. I raise a finger, tracing the tender peak of flesh above her ribs. With hungry hands, I cup her breasts, soft as dumplings. A feverish groan stirs in my throat as I squeeze them. I can't stop now, not when the aching mystery of her nipples is within my reach.

Terrible thoughts arouse me. I'm all alone with her body. I could take myself in hand, all the way to the brink. No one would ever know if I took a secret pleasure. I peel the starfish from her breasts, revealing her taut nipples, a maddening shade of pink.

She stares at me, her sky-blue eyes frozen open, haunting me with a sad kind of beauty. Something blessedly sweet washes over me, clearing my head. I yank my hands away, begging for forgiveness. After several troubled breaths, I kneel beside her, inspecting the mortal wound below her navel. If a shark was responsible, it would've left a jagged bite, but the slice is clean as a whistle.

Ivor was right. There's something peculiar about her, the same as the other cloven women who washed ashore, each with luscious lips and rivers of hair. I haven't the foggiest where such beautiful women come from. Perhaps Kilda snatches them from other isles and give them to the bluebeards for their own wicked pleasures. I hang my head in shame, scolding myself for giving into temptation.

Suddenly, the sand sings, drawing me closer to her body. I press my ear to her lips and feel her mouth moving, but how can that be? She’s long dead, and the dead don’t speak. Still, she tries to tell me her secrets. Then another sound comes, scraping and scratching. I tilt her head back and tug on her lower lip. A ghost crab skitters out of her mouth, sending a chill down my spine. I inspect the back of her throat, only to find a flap of flesh where her tongue should be.

As I trudge back to Ivor, icy raindrops pour from the sky, and the wind chops me to the bone. I huff under my breath. The weather is as petulant as Lorna.

“There’s nothing more we can accomplish now, Ivor. We’ve got a rough ride ahead, and candletime is upon us.”

Ivor nods. “What a ghastly sight: a woman split in half. I don’t think I’ll sleep a wink tonight.”

“Did you notice her tongue was severed?”

“No. I could hardly stand to look at her. I don’t know how you do it, Diarmid. Inspecting corpses and hunting murderers. Surely it wears on your nerves. Don’t you wish for a moment of peace or comfort?”

I lift my eyes to the sea cliffs, remembering Lord Goldie and his castle. “Justice is a comfort of its own.”

# 12

## Senga

On the eve of the rising moon, I prepare a sheep for my father. It's a pleasant time to be outside, crisp as the first breath of autumn. Chilly light peeks through the clouds, the scent of damp leaves and spiced mud filling the air. I'm knee-deep in the sheep pen, teetering on a stool, when the raven swoops down beside me.

He's not just any raven, but the same one who's been visiting me since I was a child. I can't be sure, but I think my grandfather sends him to me from beyond the grave. I can easily tell him apart from all the others; he has the dreariest eyes and one wing shorter than the other.

I check his beak, but it's empty. Sometimes, the raven comes without a message just to cheer me. He flits over to the sheep, and they all watch as I sharpen the blade. The old sheep are wise; they can't be swayed with a handful of grass. They clench their stubborn jaws, digging their hooves into the ground.

The young ones are much easier to tempt. Rather than pick one, I'll let one come to me. I shut my eyes and stretch out my arm. In no time at all, a rough tongue tickles my hand. I snap to attention, only to find a gentle ewe standing before me. She's barely grown, with her delicate coat and clumsy legs. My heart aches for her, but I must obey my father. I grab the scruff of her neck, and she yields without a fight, gazing up at me with big yellow eyes.

I tell myself I'm not doing anything wrong; I'm only shearing her. But *why* am I shearing her?

Because a sheared sheep is easier to slaughter.

*Slaughter*. The word sounds every bit as vicious as its meaning. I feel faraway, much like the raven when he takes flight, all feathers and wings, fuzzy edges and blue skies. I clutch the blade, trying to steady my hands. Heavens and stars, it's too late. I pierce the poor sheep and blood bubbles on her neck. I try to comfort her, but she glares at me, bleating herself into a tizzy.

Maybe some monsters aren't monsters at all, or at least they don't mean to be. Maybe they're just like me – birds falling from their nests, their thoughts flying from the cages of their bodies – and they don't realize they've slipped until they hear the bleat.

There are so many things I don't understand. I try to make sense of it all, but I can't. Abilene has human legs now, but she didn't when I first saw her. Time is strange, ebbing and flowing. I swim between the isles of now and then, clinging to a memory in the cold water.

*My first mooring on Crescent Isle.*

It was an overcast morning, clouds threatening to spill. My father and I bobbed in the lugger while my mother waited for us in The Blackhouse, sick with a wee bundle in her belly. My father warned me of the dangers that lurk in The Glass Shallows, like the stonefish that killed his father when I was just a little girl. My father steered hard for the southern tip. It wasn't particularly safe, but it was better than the western shore with its coral reef and the eastern shore with its wicked whirlpool.

Despite my father's efforts, a mighty current pulled us towards Venom Bight. I spotted Abilene before my father. I was drawn to her like a moth to a flame as she glided through the water. With icy eyes, she met my gaze, her jaw cracked open, ready to sing.

My father covered his ears. "Don't let her charm you. Plug your ears," he warned.

I did as he said, but it was no match for Abilene. The air was alive with her song, a symphony of scales and bones. Wondrous fear prickled down my neck, sending a cold splash through my veins. I felt the punch before it landed, the sting before it bit.

"Hell's bells!" my father shouted as a monstrous wave battered us.

Up from the deep, a silver-tailed mermaid clawed at us, desperate to capsize our lugger. I was afraid, but my father wasn't. Cat and mouse was his favourite game. He called on Kilda, and she steadied our lugger and made us right as rain. He thrust his arms into the water and stabbed the silver-tailed mermaid with the blubber fork. She screeched like a sea bat and plunged underwater, leaving a trail of bloody foam on the waves.

My father fell to his knees, his chest heaving, then he pointed at Abilene. "She's the one we need. Help me catch her, Senga."

I set my sights on Abilene and steered the lugger towards the shore, trapping her in The Glass Shallows. A smile bloomed on my lips as she floated over the blood-red reef. She was the most beautiful creature I'd ever seen, with hair pink as petals, creamy skin, and iridescent nipples. She was simply breathtaking.

"What are you waiting for, Senga? Grab her by the throat!" my father shouted.

Panic seized me. I couldn't move a muscle. I never meant to trap her, and now she was in danger.

My father lunged at Abilene. With a wild snort, he captured her with the ghost rope. I couldn't see it, but I heard it whipping in the wind. Abilene caught hold of his arm and sank her fangs deep. She fought against the ghost rope with all her might, but my father managed to pull her into the lugger. She flopped wildly, trying to break free, but it only made him angrier.

A vicious wave sent me flailing towards the stern. I thudded on the deck, hugging my knees to my chest. I watched helplessly as my father bloodied Abilene's nose and twisted the ghost rope tighter around her body. She gazed up at me, her eyes a startling shade of blue, a wall of ice I couldn't break through.

When we returned to The Blackhouse, my father lashed me with the harp strings. "You're a bluebeard, Senga, and you better start acting like one. You're a huntress, whether you like it or not.

Stalking is in your blood. I want to hear you say it!"

"Stalking is in my blood." I repeated the words over and over, but all I could think about was poor Abilene trapped in The Hutch.

All through the night, I heard the salt of her hiss as Kilda wicked away her fins and scales, cobbling her into something she was never meant to be – a creature who looked like me.

# 13

## Abilene

How long have I been screaming? My throat is bloody-raw, my head a constant throb. I've never been so thirsty. I lick my lips, bone-dry and split open. I feel like a smashed squid, all stringy guts and twisted limbs. My belly simmers to a boil; a flame climbs up my throat. I heave violently, spewing globs of crab and kelp.

Pain carves me like a knife. A stonefish must've stung me. It happened once before when I was a little mermaid.

I try to force my lids open, but my right eye is stuck shut. I rake my left eye through the dark. Where am I? Where's the rush of water? The rainbow of fish? The click of whales? The Hall of Mirrors?

*Where are my sisters?*

My fingers creep south, seeking golden scales, but they're gone. How can it be? A pair of legs, real human legs, smooth and long, and a curious slit between my thighs that tickles when I touch it.

I'm not naked as I was in the sea. Something awful clings to me. I scratch wildly at the cotton-stiff gown, but I can't get rid of the itch. I'm trapped in the belly of the earth with all its peculiar smells, thick with baked dirt and stale air.

In the space of a breath, it all comes rushing back to me. The Mooring and the bluebeards. The blubber fork and the ghost rope. The Glass Shallows and the bloody reef. Kilda's dark little magic. And the strange girl they call Senga, with emerald eyes – the same color I've seen in my dreams.

I reach for my silver-spun mirror, but it's not here. Each of my sisters has a special amulet. Earie has the hag stone, Florie the old eel. Fairah has the death ornament, Orla the touch, and I have the mirror. I hope I can find it and show it to Senga before it's too late.

Dawn breaks. A cone of light spills through a hole in the ground. I'm starving for salty sea air. I miss the puff of my breath underwater, fangs and scales, and trails of bubbles. Desperate to escape, I weep and wail, clawing at loose rocks until my nails rip off.

Vibrations shatter above me. Senga's father is coming; I hear his hoofbeats in the mud, his fingers rattling the latch. Then a burst of light blinds me, and I smell his sour breath on my neck.

# 14

## Senga

Foundations are hard to ignore. Ours is crooked, and it lets me know. Every day, I walk on the ashes of my grandfather and the dirt-sky of Abilene's prison. When it rains, the ground smells of faded glory, and the earth echoes with songs of old battles, old wounds, and old creatures.

But there's a silver lining in my world of grey. It's Friday, my favourite day of the week. My mother has been too sick to take Abilene to The Tide Pools, so I've been helping my father this season. Though he could easily take Abilene himself, he insists I come along with him.

And I know why.

*The shift*. My father doesn't want to be there when *it* happens, lest he succumb to one of Abilene's spells.

I keep a close eye on my father. He's in a particularly foul mood this morning. Snarling, he ties the ghost rope around Abilene's waist and binds her wrists. She flicks her tongue, returning his snarl with a hiss.

"Get over here, Senga," my father orders.

I rush to his side, but I'm not much help. Try as I might, I can't see the ghost rope. My father fastens the ghost rope to Ash's bridle. Ash is such a handsome pony, grey and sleek. Even when I pat him ever so gently, he still shrinks away from me. My father's whip has made Ash a timid creature. I feel sorry for him; I know how badly it hurts to be lashed. I think of the harp strings, and my blood runs cold. Rubbing the scars on my back, I glance at my father, but he doesn't seem to notice.

"Do you know why I fastened the ghost rope to Ash?" my father asks.

"To make sure the sea hag can't escape," I answer, eager to please him. Truth be told, I hate calling her *the sea hag*, but my father forbids me to call her a mermaid. He says it's too soft a word for so harsh a creature.

As we trudge down the sea cliffs, my thoughts drift with the clouds. I hope Abilene doesn't try anything rash today. I don't think she'll take the risk, not with her belly bulge. I can't bear the thought of her ending up like the ragdoll mermaid who went thumping down the sea cliffs three seasons ago.

I didn't know her by her name, only by her eyes, the palest blue I'd ever seen. She tried to twist herself free from the ghost rope, but her movements only made it worse. She fell from the saddle with a blood-curdling scream. She reached for Ash's haunches, trying to pull herself upright, but my father's whip kept Ash out of reach. When I close my eyes, I can still see her trembling by The Tide Pools with a bloody nose and cracked ribs.

I blink the grim image away. I follow Abilene like a shadow, savoring the smell of sage and lilies in her hair.

My father narrows his eyes at me. "If the sea hag gives you any trouble, just whistle like I showed you."

Abilene glares at my father. "Does Senga know I'm to be sacrificed for her? Does she know *why* you call it The Feast of the Singing Wound?"

"Why?" I ask.

"Because when your father chops off my tail and rips out my tongue, my wounds will sing. Even after Kilda devours me, my wounds will sing on," Abilene hisses.

"You better shut your mouth or I'll rip your tongue out now," my father snarls, jerking Abilene by the arm. "Don't listen to her, Senga. You can't believe a word she says. Sea hags are vile creatures, and we're better off without them."

At The Tide Pools, my father slings a crude spear over my shoulder. *The blubber fork*, he calls it. Once I'm armed to his satisfaction, he heads north of Wulver Cove to fish near Ivor's croft. I hope their paths don't cross. If they do, it's sure to end in a scuffle.

I wait until the fog swallows my father, then I help Abilene undress. She stands before me, stark naked on her clumsy webbed feet. Perhaps I should be afraid of her, but I'm not.

The moment Abilene steps into the water, magic swells all around her. I'm forbidden to watch the shift, but the suspense is more than I can bear. My breath hitches as I peek through the lattice of my fingers. What a thrilling sight – legs melting, hips tapering into a tail, scales blooming like golden petals.

I don’t believe in Kilda the way my family does, but I believe in Abilene in all her naked glory. On bended knee, I worship her ice-blue eyes and iridescent nipples. I rub my own rosebuds until they harden, drowning in a sea of strange feelings I can’t name.

Abilene tilts her chin to the sky, floating on her back. The ghost rope ribbons around her. I can’t see it, but she says it’s there, tethering her to the land. She dips underwater. I know she can’t escape, but with each passing second, my heart hammers as I wait for her to surface. I pucker my lips, ready to whistle for my father, when suddenly my toes prickle.

I yank my feet out of the water. “That tickles!”

Abilene emerges, rubbing her swollen belly. “I must tickle your toes while I can. My little fry won’t have feet like yours.”

“You’re on the nest like my mother, aren’t you?”

Abilene flicks her tongue and smiles.

“Who’s the father?”

“My beloved Zale. He must be worried sick about me. Have you ever loved someone?”

I blush, my thoughts awash with Ivor. “Maybe.”

“How old are you?”

“I’ll be eighteen tomorrow.”

“Why, you’re brand-new. You don’t even have a wrinkle on your face,” she croons.

“Have you and Zale been in the pink yet?” I blurt out.

Abilene tips her head back, dissolving into laughter. “*In the pink*? What the devilfish do you mean?”

“You know,” I blush. “Have you let his eel inside you?”

“How do you think my belly got so big?”

“Being in the pink makes your belly swell?”

“Sometimes.” Abilene snags a blenny and lays it flat on her tongue. It wriggles in her mouth for a second before giving up its ghost.

“I’ve never even been kissed. Do you remember your first kiss?” I ask.

“Of course. I could never forget Freya. She’s the most beautiful mermaid I’ve ever seen, with snow-white hair and eyes gold as the sun. She wasn’t born in these waters. She came from The Stark Sea with her mother. They were only passing through on their way to The Bright Sea, but I would’ve married her if she’d stayed here.”

“So, you kiss mermaids *and* mermen?”

“Naturally, but humans wouldn’t understand. Finfolk don’t have rules for who to love. We fall in love easily: with a touch, a smile, a song, a laugh, a story, a scar, a tear. It doesn’t matter who they are, only how they make us feel.”

“What made you fall in love with Zale?”

“The hole in his forearm. When I stuck my finger through it, his wound sang to me, and I felt his memories. I felt him swimming in The Glass

Shallows, fighting the current with all his might as it pulled him towards Venom Bight. I even felt the zing of the fire coral that burned clean through his forearm."

"Zale's not the only one with a scar," I observe, pointing to a trail of teeth marks along her shoulder blade.

"A goblin shark nearly shred me to the bone when I was visiting my sister Earie in The Octopus Lair." Abilene swims closer, casting her bright eyes on me. "Earie is the queenfish, you know. She's the one your family searches for every summer. Kilda wants to capture her so she can steal The Deep Dark Nether from us."

"What's *The Deep Dark Nether*?"

"It's a beautiful place at the bottom of the ocean. It's where we go when we die," Abilene answers dreamily.

"If Kilda is so powerful, then why does she need my family to capture your sister? Why doesn't she capture Earie herself?"

"What a clever question. Now you're thinking like a mermaid," Abilene croons. "Kilda needs your family because she's not nearly as powerful as she would have you believe."

"Why hasn't my family captured Earie yet?"

"Because we've done everything in our power to protect her, even sacrificing ourselves in her place. Besides, your family doesn't know what Earie looks like."

"What does she look like?"

“Wouldn’t you love to know? Then you could tell your family and help them slay our queenfish.”

“I would never do that,” I whisper, but my words don’t provide much solace. With the blubber fork strapped to my shoulders, I understand her apprehension.

Abilene eyes it scornfully. “Why don’t you put that wretched thing away and swim with me?”

I disarm myself and sink into The Tide Pools. The water sparkles, brisk and blue, as I cup it in my hands. I feel so free, as though I’ve sprouted wings. Abilene chases a ghost crab, her fingers snapping like a trap. I close my eyes. The world is a splash of sounds. A breath later, I feel her fingers creeping along my collarbone.

“What a pretty black pearl,” she whispers, touching the rosette in the hollow of my throat. “Did your father give it to you?”

“No, Ivor gave it to me. He’s the only friend I’ve ever had.”

“Ivor must think you’re something special. Black pearls are hard to find. I bet he dove a thousand times to find such a treasure.”

“Heavens and stars, I had no idea the trouble he went to.”

Abilene snags another blenny. “Do you know why some pearls turn black?”

I shake my head, raising a curious brow.

“Because something terrible slips inside the oyster and wounds it. Oysters feel pain just like we do. They even cry like we do. Their tears are what turns pearls black." Her voice rivers around me, rushing deep. I close my eyes, dipping my head on her shoulder. "But oysters fight back," Abilene hisses, running her fingers through my hair. "I know who you are, Senga. You're a black pearl from The Bitter Sea. Something terrible has slipped inside you, but you're fighting back."

# 15

## Senga

When the moon is full, my family honors Kilda with smoke and flames. I bow my head and whisper the words my father wants to hear. I don't want to pray, but it's the only way to avoid another lashing.

*Kilda Almighty, hear our prayer. Anoint us with the sap of your branches and wash us in your dark little magic.*

I wipe the false prayer from my lips, glancing over at the stone slab drenched in blood. At once, I recognize the sheep; it's the gentle ewe I sheared last week. Her carcass lies on the altar, her bones glittering in the rain. My eyes drift to the splitting block, where her skull hangs from a stake. I stare at the slain creature, looking for a trace of forgiveness, but there is none to be found. She curses me with her limp tongue instead.

The westerly winds blow, souring the air with curdled blood and snapped tendons. I pinch my nose, turning my attention to something else, *anything* else. Raindrops falling, soft and steady. Flames spitting and burning out. Petrels piping in the treetops. The ground crisp with amber leaves.

I flick my eyes at my mother. "Do we have to sacrifice the sea hag? The poor thing is on the nest like you are."

Naturally, my father takes it upon himself to speak for her. "A belly bulge is no reason to spare the sea hag."

"I was talking to *mother*."

Gunn grabs me by the wrist, his eyes landing on my lips. “You’ve got a mouth on you. You shouldn’t talk to your father that way.”

Lorna rubs his shoulders, swaying him to release me. “Oh, come now. Senga isn’t a little girl anymore. She’s swum in the river of blood, and women are allowed to have their own opinions.”

“I know nothing about the river of blood, nor do I wish to,” Gunn snorts, mead dribbling down his chin.

“Could we sacrifice another sea hag instead?”

“Listen to me, Senga,” Lorna says sharply. “Kilda has delivered us, and we must glorify her. The pregnant sea hag in The Hutch is a miracle. We have one sea hag for you and one for the wee bundle in your mother’s belly.”

My heart skips a beat. Abilene was telling the truth after all. My family *does* sacrifice mermaids for me on The Feast of the Singing Wound. A familiar feeling washes over me, slippery and faraway. My ears ring, red edges all around me, a smear of blood and flames.

My mother garbles, but I can’t make sense of it. Paling, she whips her head around, emptying her belly. Then she wipes the spit from her mouth and returns to knitting.

I touch her shoulder. “Are you alright?”

My mother cowers in the firelight, looking lost and wounded. I can’t fathom her being brave enough to defy my father, but she did the day I was born. She's the only reason I'm alive, and perhaps I'm the reason she suffers.

Lorna prances around the fire, her hair flowing like honey. "I daresay we've captured the queenfish. Surely the pregnant sea hag is the one Kilda has been searching for."

"I doubt she's the queenfish. Of all the sea hags, what are the odds she's the one?" I question.

"What would you know about the queenfish?" Lorna scoffs. She looks over at my father and Gunn. "By the cold moon of Hogmanay, we'll be gods, just as Kilda promised. How splendid it'll be to summon the waves and conjure the wind, or set fire to anything my heart desires, or fly through the heavens on silk wings. Just imagine Kilda's delight when we bring her the queenfish and a finling."

My father grins with a jumble of teeth. "Kilda loves sweetmeats. She'll swallow the finling whole."

Gunn makes a slurping sound, causing my belly to roil.

"Come hither, my little thistle. I'm worried about you," Lorna says, her voice caught between a snarl and a whisper. "Has the sea hag been sending you dreams?"

"No. It just doesn't seem right to sacrifice her when she's pregnant."

"The sea hag is our enemy, Senga," my father snorts. "Don't ever lose sight of that, or Kilda will punish you. I know you're some kind of water witch like your mother; I've known it from the moment you were born with that slimy caul on your head. But you're still my daughter, and blood is thicker than water. There's not a chance in blazes we're setting that devilfish free, especially after all the trouble it took to catch her." He scowls at me, stomping his boots on the ground.

My father and Gunn have never taken their boots off in front of me, not even after a long day's work as they recline by the fire. I'm afraid of what hides underneath. Perhaps they really *do* have hooves for feet.

Lorna fixes her cruel eyes on me. "Your father is right. It seems you've forgotten that blood is thicker than water. Perhaps a gut bath will help you remember where your loyalty lies."

"No, Lorna, please," I cry.

"Strip down and sit by the fire. I'm in no mood to argue," Lorna hisses. She saunters off to grab a bucket, her dress swishing behind her.

I peel off my clothes, cursing my fingers for moving against my will. Soon, I'm sitting by the fire, cross-legged and naked. I imagine the needle and thread, stitching my legs together, hiding my honeypot, sealing up all the secrets inside me.

My father looks away. My mother gags again. The brownie spies on me from the hawthorn tree, and Gunn drags his big eyes over my body. I want to yank the silver horn from his hand and bash his skull in with it.

Lorna looks down at me, then tips the bucket, bathing me in organs and entrails. The liver is slick and fat as it slides between my breasts. The heart comes next, with its phantom pulse of arteries. A hoof hits my head, sticking to the gory mess in my hair.

I squeeze the black pearl around my neck, seeking comfort. I wish Ivor was here with me, not to save me, but to wrap his arms around me, to hide my naked body, to feel what I feel. The tang of iron and blood. The mush of membranes. The drip of veins painting me red. But Ivor's not here. He's with Mina MacTavish in their marriage bed.

My body simmers like a teapot. Something cracks inside me, and my spine goes soft like pudding. The steam escapes and the pressure melts away as Abilene's words swim through my heart.

*Something terrible has slipped inside you, but you're fighting back.*

Something terrible *has* slipped inside me, but I *am* fighting back. Courage is a muscle, and mine is growing stronger. I smile, hugging my knees to my chest, scales blooming on my legs.

# 16

## Senga

Abilene sings to me in The Tide Pools, her tail gleaming harp-gold. Her voice is the prettiest instrument I've ever heard. Pleasure washes over me in little licks of joy.

Without warning, Abilene snaps her mouth shut, and the song is gone. She looks at me, our eyes locking. "Sometimes, I hear a man singing when I'm in The Hutch. There's so much water in his voice – enough to drown me, were I not a mermaid. I pretend it's Zale coming to save me and my little fry."

"Maybe it *is* Zale."

"It's not Zale," she says gloomily.

"I bet it's the brownie!"

"No, it's not the brownie either."

"Then who is it?" I ask impatiently, swishing my hands through the water.

"Probably a wulver. Such handsome creatures, with chiseled jaws and strapping shoulders. The wulvers used to sing me and my sisters to sleep. A few of them sang even more beautifully than I do." Abilene winks at me like a proper human, and with her tail underwater, I almost forget she's a mermaid.

"My father says I'm supposed to run if I see a wulver. He says they're savage beasts who stalk Wulver Cove, seeking revenge."

"Your father has every right to fear them."

"What do you mean?"

Abilene lifts a finger, pointing at the sea caves glinting red in the sun. "The wulvers used to live there. You've met them before. You just don't remember. When you were born, your mother nursed you in the sea caves, did she not?"

"Yes. Ivor told me on Hogmanay last year."

"Well, before your father came along, the landies lived in harmony with the wulvers. Your grandfather even thought of them as friends. They howled at the moon and bathed in the sea together, but then a terrible thing happened."

I shiver. "What happened?"

"Not long after the bluebeards captured Hourglass Isle, a young wulver overheard them talking about their covenant with Kilda."

"What did the wulver do?"

"He dashed to the sea caves, pressed his lips to the water, and summoned us. He warned us about The Mooring, The Feast of the Singing Wound, and the bluebeards' plan to hunt us."

"I wish I could be as brave as him," I say, the words leaving a bitter taste in my mouth

"When Kilda learned of the wulver's kindness to us, she ordered the bluebeards to slay his family." Abilene frowns, lowering her voice. "It was your father who mangled the wulver's eye."

The wind snarls, threatening to snap the sturdiest of trees. An image of Ivor burns through the fog, and my heart skips a beat. What if he's the wulver from the story? What if he's only pretending to be my friend? A wave of nausea hits me. Stifling a gag, I rub the rosette in the hollow of my throat.

Abilene swims closer, casting her eyes like nets. "What's the matter? Cat got your tongue?"

"Ivor has a dead eye," I say in a strangled tone.

Her lips curve into a smile. "I know."

"But Ivor isn't a wulver. He looks just like me and the other landies, apart from the ink on his skin."

"Appearances are tricky. Kilda's dark little magic has muddled your mind."

"I think you're the one who's trying to trick me. Wulvers are just legends from long ago," I sulk, crossing my arms.

"And what about me? Am I a legend from long ago?" Abilene hisses, roping me with her tail. "One of us is the truth and the other an illusion. What if I'm the truth and you're an illusion?"

My eyes fly open, sparking with anger. "I don't believe you. You're lying to me. You're a devilfish, a witch, just like my father said!"

Abilene tilts her chin, looking heavenward. "There's no such thing as witches. Only women who embrace their true nature."

An urge seizes me: to cause Abilene pain. My father thinks I lack the instinct, but I'm a huntress through and through. I want to break her collarbone. Scrape the edge of her liver. Gouge the tender grooves between her ribs. The blubber fork rises from the mist, its barbed edges walking on water, tempting me to ram it into Abilene's fork-tender skin. Right through the heart should do the trick, or perhaps I'm in the mood for something more sinister. Perhaps I should ram it right into her belly bulge.

I bite my lip, resisting the awful impulses. "Why must you torment me? I thought we were friends."

"I'm not trying to torment you. I'm trying to help you, but sometimes it hurts to be helped." Abilene sighs, peeling a starfish from her breast. Her bare nipple shines bright as the moon, and I want to lick it. "You can't see the ghost rope that binds me, can you?"

"No."

"But you believe me when I say it's there?"

"Yes."

"Well, just as you can't see the ghost rope that binds me, perhaps you can't see Ivor's true nature – or your own. Before The Great Divide, your ancestors were eternals. There were many clans, but one spirit."

Abilene is charming me, swaddling me in a spell just like my father said she would. But I'm stronger than her, and I can't let her push me around. I dig my feet into a rock ledge and stand my ground. "You're just playing tricks on me," I say scornfully.

"Listen to me, angelfish. Kilda's dark little magic is a disease that has ravaged your isle. You can't see clearly, but I can." Abilene waves her hands, and a silver-spun mirror appears. It floats above the water, just out of my reach.

Suddenly, my father chops through the fog. He waves his axe at us, and I skitter away from her.

"Senga Thistle! You know better than to talk to that devilfish. She'll poison your mind. How many times do I have to tell you?" he scolds me, lugging a net of hake over his shoulder.

"I was warning her about the blubber fork," I lie.

"Cover her up at once. A squall is coming." He pushes past us, hightailing it to The Blackhouse.

I dress Abilene in the shabby stay she's worn since the day we captured her. Fright-sick and positively in love, I wink at her, and she charms my ears with her silent song in return. I'm glad my father is in front of us. I don't want him to see me floating lighter than air, grinning from ear to ear.

As we round the sandstone bluffs, high above the sea, I'm still intoxicated by her voice. Behind a soft curtain of clouds, the sun sheds its blood, and the sea rolls gold with frenzy.

Once we return home, my mother waddles outside, shielding herself from the pouring rain.

My father shouts at her. "Is The Hutch ready for the sea hag?"

My mother nods.

"Good. Now, go back inside before you catch a cold. You must keep our son healthy, Twila." His words stab me, blade on bone. I know how badly my father wants a son. "You get inside too, Senga. Help your mother with supper, and don't forget to leave a treat for the brownie."

I do as he says, dragging my feet inside. I sit beside my mother at the table, helping her roll the tatties into tiny cakes. The bloody-black walls haunt me, gaping like open wounds. I try to forget about The Hutch, the ghost rope, and Ivor's dead eye, but The Feast of the Singing Wound is on the horizon, tearing its way through the dismal sky.

Heavens and stars, I almost forgot the honeycomb. It's the brownie's favourite. When I swing the door open, I feel him waiting on me. I can't see him, of course, but I toss him the golden brittle all the same. His cobwebs cling to me as I swat them away. No matter how much I sweep and dust and douse the cobwebs, they cleave to our Blackhouse. The brownie weaves his web like a spider, and I'm the fly caught in the middle.

# 17

## Abilene

The Hutch is sharp as coral and tight as a shelf in Shimmer Cave. I catch a shallow breath, my lungs hissing in pain. There's a song on the tip of my tongue, but I can't remember how to sing.

Kilda haunts me in the muddy sludge where water meets earth, strangling me with her gnarled roots. Her heart beats underground, echoing mine. As I press my ear to the dirt, another sound breaks loose, so faint I can barely hear it. The cry of singing wounds. Who does it belong to? Perhaps it's one of my long-lost sisters, or a poor ghost on this isle.

Then I think of *her*, touching my belly, a tear rolling down my cheek.

My little fry is so fragile. I fear she might break, shatter like a mirror inside me, reflecting all my sharp edges. I dare not move a muscle. I wear my body skintight, but my spirit fins for open water. I drift softly through rings of blue, a jellyfish stinging through space and time.

I snag a memory. Squeeze it in my hand. It squirms like a moon snail. I swallow it, feel it aching in my throat. It smells of seaweed and damp bones: the salty taste of home.

Gran Opal is there in the memory, her face a weathered seashell. My sisters are there too, wrapping their tails around me. Gran Opal is the wisest eternal in these waters, but the sand in her hourglass is almost spent. I smell the rot on her breath as she sings an old, sad song. Humans prattle on and on, but Gran Opal only sings on special occasions. She's saving her voice for The Deep Dark Nether, where she can sing all through the night and all through the ages.

Gran Opal smooths a hand over her bone-white hair. She nudges Orla, giving her a sly wink. Orla is the wisest of my sisters. She was born with *the touch*, and soon she'll take Gran Opal's place, stirring The Cauldron and conjuring storms with her fingers.

"Tell your sisters the story of creation," Gran Opal bids.

Orla graces us with a smile, flipping her ruby fins eagerly. "Before The Great Divide, there was no separation between creatures. We were all eternals, equal parts god and human, and though we were many clans, we were one spirit. It was a glorious time, when all creatures, great and small, sang of blood and sand together. But then our sister Kilda tricked herself into thinking she could become something greater, so she sacrificed her heart – the very thing that made her human – so she could become a pure god." Orla pauses, a shadow darkening her expression. She draws a long bubbly breath before continuing. "Ever since that fateful night, Kilda has been bound to The Brittle Forest. Her dark little magic has poisoned Hourglass Isle, and the humans have forgotten their true nature."

I flick my tongue at Gran Opal, summoning my courage. "Are humans dangerous?"

"Yes, very, for they often destroy what they don't understand," Gran Opal hisses, crunching on a barnacle. "And there will soon come a day when even Crescent Isle won't be safe for us anymore."

"Why?" we chime in unison.

"Because the bluebeards of The Minch are about to wake, and, when they do, they'll make a covenant with Kilda, and they'll hunt us during The Mooring every summer."

"Why does Kilda need the bluebeards?" I ask.

"Because they're the only ones who can catch the queenfish. That's why we must protect our queenfish at The Mooring, even if it means sacrificing ourselves. She's our only hope for immortality. Without her, we'll lose The Deep Dark Nether."

Florie splashes her silver tail, her clever eyes gleaming. "The bluebeards can't catch us or our queenfish if we're not there. Do we really have to go to The Mooring?"

"Yes," Gran Opal swishes. "We must take our chances at The Mooring, for it's written in the skin of the sea. We can't escape The Mooring; we can only endure it. Kilda caused The Great Divide, and we must atone for her wicked deeds. Better a few of us die than all of us lose The Deep Dark Nether. When you feel your courage waning, you must remember who you are," Gran Opal sages, polishing us with her wisdom.

"Who are we?" we chime in unison.

"You're angelfish on high, protectors of The Deep Dark Nether," Gran Opal croons.

My sisters and I stretch out on a rock ledge, our gaze drifting to Shimmer Cave. We haven't been inside yet. A giant boulder blocks the entrance, and Gran Opal is the only one with the power to move it. But The Jubilee is coming, and soon our queenfish will be of age. Until then, we're forbidden to enter Shimmer Cave, for the hag stone sleeps inside, and Gran Opal has been casting her dreams upon it for centuries.

We swim through Gran Opal's eyes, a living reef of rainbows. Her emerald eye thrills me, like a dip in the seafloor where the water is ice-warm.

A moment later, my youngest sister skims into the light. Earie is nothing short of hideous, her face a gory melt of flesh and bones. She resembles a sputtering candle or a smudged portrait. And yet, she's a thing of wonder: violet eyes and ink-black hair. Tentacles laced with venom and a rack of coral antlers.

I dodge a tentacle as Earie swims past me. She bows before Gran Opal and waits a breath before whispering, "Why does Kilda torture me so?"

"Because you're our queenfish and you're the only one who can inherit The Deep Dark Nether," Gran Opal swishes.

"Then why don't I welcome death now? The sooner the better," Earie hisses, her voice a shiver in the night. "I've imagined a thousand ways to die. It would be so easy. I could slit my wrists with sea glass and bleed myself dry. I could pick a fight with the saw-toothed sharks. I could swim above the salt and sing to the lonely sailors."

"Earie, my angelfish," Gran Opal whispers. "You know time must run its course. A natural death is the only path to The Deep Dark Nether."

Earie snaps her violet eyes shut, tears glittering down her cheeks. Her body is a secret garden where things go to die, with spikes and thorns around every corner. She swats at her tentacles as they bloom around her. "None of you know the horror of living in my body. I'd rather be dead than have Kilda's curse upon me."

Gran Opal swims closer, curling her tail around Earie. "What is a curse but an illusion of power? A miracle could be yours, if you twist the pain in your favor."

"But I don't want the pain. I don't want these mushy candle bones or these wretched tentacles. I want to rise above the salt and live on Hourglass Isle. I want to be a human or a god like Kilda. Maybe then, she'd stop torturing me. I just want Kilda to love me," Earie cries, inking the sea with her shame. Her tentacles cackle at her confession, grinding their spiny teeth together.

Gran Opal lifts Earie's crooked chin until their eyes meet. "Behold my amber eye. One day, you'll see this eye in another. It will cause you more joy and more pain than you could ever imagine, but in the end, it'll set you free, and that's all that matters."

Earie stares deep into the amber eye, her tentacles quieting.

"We all dream of ways to escape our pain, but the truth remains: humans are illusions, and Kilda will never love you, no matter what you do," Gran Opal sages. "But if you honor your true nature and bear the burden of your tentacles, then you'll inherit The Deep Dark Nether for yourself and your sisters. The choice is yours to make, but whatever you choose, you must choose it with all your heart."

A hush washes over the sea. On tails and needles we wait, our lungs a tight squeeze. Orla rubs the pearls around her neck. Florie digs her nails into my shoulders, painting the water fright-red. I cringe, hoping the goblin sharks don't smell the blood.

"Do you wish to join Kilda above the salt?" Gran Opal asks.

"No," Earie replies with resolve.

"Do you wish to be a human or a god?"

"No. I don't wish to be anything but a mermaid. I trust in our true nature," Earie says, holding her head high.

Gran Opal softens, affection warming her cheeks. "Earie, my angelfish, your tentacles may be wretched now, but one black and blessed night, they'll be our salvation. If you die in good graces, honoring your true nature, The Deep Dark Nether will be ours and ours alone. Kilda will turn to dust, and you'll sing our bones eternal."

We chant and chime, beating our tails against the fire coral.

*Sing we angelfish on high.*
*Sing we of The Deep Dark Nether.*
*Sing our tongues of blood and sand.*
*Sing our bones eternal.*

Gran Opal croons along with us until her six eyes droop. "I'm afraid I'm waning. I don't know how humans prattle on all day. It's exhausting." She tilts her head back with a yawn. "Does anyone have a burning question before I retire?"

"I do," Fairah pipes up, licking her poppy-red lips.

Fairah is my eldest sister and the fairest of us all, with sky-blue eyes and long cinnamon braids. As I stare at her, I feel like a lovelorn human stranded on the rocks of her beauty. Even Gran Opal is smitten by her, all hips and breasts and tingly sensations. All the merman desire her; one has already stuck his eel inside her and tickled her gills.

"I promise to protect Earie at The Mooring, even if it means sacrificing myself," Fairah vows, pressing a hand to her heart. "But shouldn't we at least try to fight back against the bluebeards?"

"What a clever question," Gran Opal grins. "Of course I want you to fight back. Fight back with all your might. Rip them from limb to limb. Fang them to death. Drown their children. Drag their luggers to the bottom of the sea. Do whatever you can to destroy them."

Fairah dances through the saltlick, her cinnamon hair swirling around her. A jade pendant gleams between her breasts, edged in the bones and the teeth of our mother. Fairah has the great honor of wearing our mother's death ornament. If I'm honest with myself, I've always been rather jealous of that.

After Gran Opal retires to her oyster bed, we propel to the surface like shooting stars, our bodies burning bright and raw. Above the salt, we float in The Glass Shallows. We're tempted to explore the rocky shores of Crescent Isle, but we must wait for The Jubilee on Earie's fifteenth birthday.

Orla bobs and weaves, her ruby tail blending in with the reef. She's the best huntress among us. Camouflaged in coral-red, she can catch the most difficult creatures. With a wild splash, she snatches a bonefish. Her mouth flies open and she flicks her tongue in satisfaction.

Florie's blonde hair shines in the sun as the old eel licks her clean. He never leaves her side. He follows her around, memories glowing in his belly like fireflies. The old eel is her amulet as the mirror is mine.

Fairah swims over to a kelp bed and sweeps her fingers under the rock ledge. Beaming, she cups an abalone in her palms, then pries the rose-red meat from its shell and swallows it whole.

As for poor Earie, the current pulls her towards Venom Bight. She wears her tentacles like a veil, holding a parasol overhead to keep from scorching in the sun. A stonefish hides between her coral antlers. I shudder at the sight.

*Stonefish.* The very word turns my blood to ice.

Long ago, under the frost moon, Earie and I were braiding each other's hair when a stonefish crept out of its nest and stung me on the neck. I was sick in my oyster bed for seventeen days while a feverish venom coursed through my veins. Racked with guilt, Earie refused to sleep with me and my sisters any longer. She made herself a new bed in The Octopus Lair, buried in the deepest trenches among the goblin sharks.

Though it pains me to see Earie go her own way, I know it's only natural. She belongs in the shivering dark with all the other rock beauties. Earie eats things I could never eat. She has a penchant for sea urchins. I've seen her swallow them whole: shells, spine, teeth, and all.

# 18

## Diarmid

Ivor grows stronger each day, while I grow weaker. He's not a bow-legged boy anymore, but a man of iron and muscles. All the fair maidens fancy him, even though he took Mina MacTavish to the marriage bed last month. Mina is a sickly bride and old as the hills, but Ivor couldn't refuse her, not after what her father did for him.

We trudge along the wind-battered beach just south of Lorna's blackhouse. We lug the skiff through the sand, Ivor shouldering the weight. I tag along behind him, feeling small, but I refuse to succumb to jealousy. Ivor is the closest thing to a friend I have on this damned isle, and I rather enjoy his company. He's a man of goodwill and honor. I can't thank him enough for helping me bring justice to Hourglass Isle, combing the shores for cloven women, settling property disagreements fairly, and keeping the peace between surly drifters in The Teahouse.

The sun sinks into the sea, spinning the water with its golden thread. Ivor lifts his spyglass, pressing his dead eye to it. "It's a good night for fishing. The squall won't blow ashore until morning."

Ivor is always right as rain about the weather. I've never doubted his dead eye, not for a single second. Huffing and puffing, we launch off into the gloaming, the violet sky washing us clean.

"I've always wanted to see a wulver," I grin, giving Ivor a playful nudge. "If you know where they're hiding, you can tell me. I promise I won't tell a soul."

Ivor casts his line in the water, his face obscured by the lengthening shadows.

*Chomp* goes the wind, biting through me. With a wild flap, a pelican swoops down, skimming the waves. In no time at all, his pouch is full of fish. My belly growls at the sight of his catch.

With a loud splash, the rod jerks. "Fish on the line!" Ivor shouts.

I fall to my knees in thanksgiving while Ivor reels in the line. I'm not sure who – or what – I'm thanking, but I'm thanking with all my heart. A wave pummels the skiff, slamming me portside. My shoulder aches, but I'm at peace. I can feed Sorcha and my children tonight.

Ivor wipes the sweat from his brow and plops the fish in my lap. "I've been having the strangest dream."

"What of?"

"The cloven woman I found last November." He pauses, all worry lines and harsh angles. "In the dream, I'm searching for her corpse. I know she's somewhere along the beach, but I can't find her. I'm in complete and utter darkness until a bright light spills from the sky and I spot her on the shore. But the moment I take a step towards her, she cobbles into a mermaid and swims away."

"A mermaid?" I repeat, filling the air with a throaty laugh.

Ivor clenches his jaw. "Oh, I see how it is. You believe in spells and wulvers and bluebeards from The Minch, but not in mermaids?"

I crack a smile. "Alright, my friend. Let's say mermaids are real. What then?"

Ivor leans into me, raising a brow. "What if the cloven women aren't *women* at all? What if they're *mermaids*? I overheard the bluebeards talking about mermaids when I was just a boy."

"What did they say?" I ask, itching for an answer.

"They made a covenant with Kilda to hunt mermaids." Ivor eyes me, gauging my reaction.

I scratch my beard in amusement. "I've always thought the cloven women were unusual. I just couldn't put my finger on it, but your theory surely would explain it."

"My father believed mermaids could cast their dreams on humans. Maybe the mermaids are appearing in my dreams to help me parse out the truth."

"Stranger things have happened," I say, chewing on my lip. Darkness descends on us, the moon a fingernail in the sky. With each passing second, Ivor's theory becomes more believable. "Perhaps the cloven women really *are* mermaids. Regardless, the bluebeards must be stopped. Their wicked ways have gone on long enough." I pound my fists on the skiff, catching a splinter on a loose plank. "Let's ride to their blackhouse tonight and interrogate them."

"Slow down, Diarmid. We need a plan first."

"I don't understand you, Ivor. The bluebeards murdered your family in cold blood. Don't you want revenge?"

"More than anything." Ivor spits the words at me.

A wiser man would hold his tongue, but hot-bellied anger spurs me on. "Then why didn't you bear witness all those years ago? Why didn't you tell everyone what you saw? Perhaps the bluebeards would've been brought to justice a long time ago."

Ivor flinches, his breath needle-thin. "I was a boy at the time, fatherless and afraid. Sir MacTavish advised me to keep my mouth shut. He said bearing witness wouldn't do any good anyways." He raises his voice, his eyes reddening. "The bluebeards rule this isle with an iron fist, and Kilda's favor is upon them. You know that as well as I do."

"I'm sorry, Ivor," I say in earnest. "Of course, you were afraid. You were just a boy who'd lost everything."

"Besides, if we ruffle their feathers, they might go after our families. Not to mention if we lock horns with them, they may take their anger out on Lorna, Twila, and Senga. I know how badly you want to be the hero who drags them to The Teahouse and serves them justice, but even *if* we shackled them, they might still find a way to escape. Kilda will be quick to help them." Ivor pauses, his dead eye flickering. "But I have an idea that might give us the advantage we need."

I flash a toothy grin. "Well, don't keep me in suspense."

"I've been hearing Senga's voice in my dreams."

I blink in surprise. "What does she say?"

"She says her family is going to The Brittle Forest at the end of October to have a feast for Kilda. Maybe there's a connection between the feast in October and the cloven women washing ashore in November."

I thump his shoulder affectionately. "Holy poker, Ivor. I think you're onto something."

"If we want to stop the bluebeards, our best chance is a surprise attack. It's half past October, and the feast for Kilda will soon be upon us. If we keep watch near Fallow Point, we might be able to catch them in the act and attack when they least expect it."

My heart thumps, craving carnage. "Attack them? Do you really mean it?"

"Yes. I want the bluebeards to pay for their wicked deeds just as much as you do." Ivor rows for the shore, gritting his teeth. "If we work together, perhaps we can finally destroy them. Can you meet me at my croft tomorrow night?"

"I'll be there with bells on." I beam. "Perhaps there's hope for me and Lorna and you and Senga after all."

“Me and Senga? Have you gone mad? I just married Mina.”

“There’s no need to be tragically sensible. You’re in good company with me. I know your marriage is one of convenience. I’ve seen the way your eyes twinkle around Senga.” I wink, nettling him.

“My eyes don’t twinkle,” he snaps.

“I can read you like a book, Ivor. I know your heart belongs to Senga.”

Ivor bristles. “Who my heart belongs to is not your concern.”

# 19

## Ivor

Once the skiff is moored, Diarmid readies his pony and rides home to Sorcha and his children. I huff out a sigh, my breath fogging in the dark. Truth be told, I'm glad to be rid of Diarmid. He has a way of stealing my peace and frazzling my nerves. The more I'm around him, the more I doubt myself and my decisions.

It's a wonder Diarmid hasn't washed ashore alongside the cloven women. He spills his guts to anyone who'll listen. He wears his heart on his sleeve and professes his love for Lorna when he has a wife and children at home. Not to mention, he openly accuses the bluebeards of murder.

Obviously, I want revenge on the bluebeards, but it's foolish to pick a fight I can't win. As much as I loathe to admit it, Diarmid is right about Mina. My marriage *is* one of convenience, but does he really expect me to say it out loud? I owe Sir MacTavish and Mina my life and more. They were the only ones who lifted a finger to help me when my family died.

As I trudge back to my croft, I bite back hot tears and rage, my heart churning with other less definable emotions. A memory tugs on the line: the night I tried to kill the bluebeards.

Light snow dusted the ground as I crept to their blackhouse with a bow on my back and a blade in my sheath, but my plans were quickly foiled. Their land was a death trap; I nearly fell into a sinkhole. When Senga heard the commotion, she tiptoed outside only to find me hobbling around on a twisted knee. She feared her father would kill me if he caught me, so she begged me to hide behind the hawthorn tree.

Just as I slipped behind the twisted trunk, Warr thundered through the front door. "Senga Thistle! What are you doing out here in the middle of the night? I told you to stop looking for the brownie!"

"I wasn't looking for the brownie, I swear. I heard a noise outside my window, but it was only an owl," Senga lied. "It's freezing cold. Let's hurry back inside."

"Who are you to give me orders?" Warr kicked up his heels and charged at her, clumps of dirt flying everywhere. She cowered down, her spirit broken, as he yanked her by the arm and hauled her into The Blackhouse.

I hid behind the hawthorn until dawn, trying to summon my courage. I wanted to beat down the door, to pounce on Warr and wring his neck, but I didn't.

To this day, I still feel like a coward. I should've protected Senga from her father, no matter the cost. And this is what Diarmid does when he speaks without thinking – drudges up old wounds and drowns me in my own suffering.

My heart pounds in my chest, but the line keeps tugging. I reel in another memory: the day my father died in the sea caves.

I knelt beside him, his face battered beyond recognition, his body splayed on a rock. He grabbed his belly, nothing but raw ribs and warm guts. Flaps of meat hung from his face, an eye dangling where his nose should have been.

My father took me by the hand, blood leaking from his eye sockets. “Be strong, my boy,” he choked.

I swallowed hard. “What should I do? I can barely draw my bow, let alone aim.”

“Just close your eyes and let the arrows fly. I’ll always be with you.”

“I’m sorry for warning the mermaids,” I whispered, blinking away the tears.

“You did the right thing, my boy. You honored our true nature. Just promise me you’ll bury me and your brothers in the sea caves before the bluebeards smoke us into burnt offerings.”

“I give you my word,” I vowed, glancing over at my brothers, their entrails tangled in a gruesome heap.

My father stared at me, the light in his eyes snuffing out. With a violent shake, he rattled his last breath. I turned away, purging my belly until there was nothing but holes left inside me.

When my father was alive, everything was so clear, but the longer I’m without him, the more muddled I feel. The earth and the sea have become cruel riddles. I used to know the difference between poison and medicine, but now I’m not sure what hurts and what heals.

An image flutters behind my eyes. I see my father bathing in the sea. Hear him howling at the moon. Feel the rough of his fur against my cheek. One thing is certain: I need to be more creaturely, like him.

I take the long way home, though Mina is waiting for me. I crouch down on all fours, rolling my shoulders forward. Old sensations pulse through me: skin and bones shifting. Muscles stretching. Fangs pricking. Fur tingling down my spine. I snap my neck back and howl at the moon, then I dash into the dark of night, crunching through amber leaves and pine needles.

# 20

## Senga

"Do you want to know a secret?" Abilene whispers, her lips grazing the shell of my ear.

I nod, her honey-sweet voice sending wingbeats through my belly.

"Before The Great Divide, Kilda was my sister."

My eyes widen. "Kilda is your sister?"

"She *was* my sister, but she's not anymore. Not after she betrayed the eternals and endangered The Deep Dark Nether. Kilda is every bit as wicked as your father. She'll stop at nothing to confuse you. She's desperate to make you believe you're human."

"Well, if I'm not human, then what am I? An eternal?" I ask incredulously.

"Yes, and so is everyone else on Hourglass Isle. That's what I've been trying to tell you." Abilene sighs with irritation. "I'm sure you've seen glimpses of your true nature, but you dismiss them. You chalk them up to figments of your imagination, tricks of the light, bouts of hysteria, tired eyes not seeing clearly." Abilene pauses, pinning me with an icy stare. "But what if those glimpses are your intuition? The wisdom inside you that knows without knowing? Kilda's not the only one with dark little magic. It's inside us all. What matters is how we use it."

I muse for a moment, flooded with images. My father's hoof-feet. Ivor's fang-toothed smile. My grandfather's peculiar whiskers. The needle and thread stitching my legs together, silver scales blossoming. "You might be right," I yield.

Abilene brightens. "I have an idea. How about I ask you some questions and you try listening to your intuition? It's not as hard as you think. Just breathe into your belly and tell me what you hear."

I close my eyes, smiling.

Abilene begins. "Is Kilda your god?"

"No, and she never will be."

"Do you believe I'm your friend?"

"Yes, with all my heart."

"Do you want to sacrifice me and my little fry?"

"No, of course not. I swear."

"Do you think your father is bad?"

"Yes, but I still love him." I hang my head in shame, my smile fading. Suddenly, I don't like this game.

"Are you lonely?"

"Yes, miserably. Kilda has bestowed her favor upon my family, but I feel cursed."

"I'm glad you're lonely," Abilene remarks. "Loneliness isn't a curse. It's a miracle. It means you feel the separation. There's hope for you yet, angelfish. Somewhere, deep down inside, you remember your true nature."

"How can you be so old and so beautiful at the same time?"

Abilene raises a brow. "Haven't you heard? Old is the best kind of beautiful." A gull swoops down and perches on her shoulder, squawking and beating his wings against her. “See, even the gull agrees with me,” she croons.

“What makes the water so blue?” I ask, nettling her with another question.

“Mermaid tears,” she hisses. “My sister Fairah sobbed in these tide pools last October. I heard her wounds singing in the wind.”

“I didn’t know we captured one of your sisters,” I whisper, looking away. I fix my eyes on The Peekaboos, counting the bleak clouds in the sky.

“Fairah isn’t the only one you captured. You captured my aunt Hella and seven of my cousins. You even captured a few mermaids from The Bright Sea. Every one of them sacrificed their lives during The Mooring so Earie might save The Deep Dark Nether, and their children might live to taste immortality. Can you imagine that kind of sacrifice?” Abilene prods, sweeping a hand under my jaw, turning me towards her.

“No,” I rasp.

“Fairah was my eldest sister. She was vibrant and beautiful, with sky-blue eyes and hair rich as cinnamon. She was captured last year at The Mooring and never returned to us. It stands to reason she was sacrificed by your family. Do you remember Fairah?”

“Not by name. You’re the first mermaid I’ve ever talked to, but she fits the description of the mermaid we captured last summer. She was the most beautiful creature I’ve ever seen, present company excluded," I swoon, reaching for Abilene's hand.

*Crack!* A storm cloud bursts, drenching us to the bone. Abilene winces, clawing the sand from her eyes. "Can't you see that me and my little fry are in danger? The Feast of the Singing Wound is coming, and your father will slay us."

"The brownie slays mermaids. Not my father."

Abilene bristles, hiding her face behind a slab of driftwood. "Does it really matter who does it? Either way, one of them will chop my tail off and rip out my tongue, and I'll be bound to the land and separated from the finfolk forever."

Abilene glides closer to me, wrapping her golden tail around me. She opens her mouth, holding the first note on her tongue just to torture me. I rake my heels against the rocks, a cold splash swimming through me. I search for my reflection in the lonely looking glass of water, but there's only Abilene – beautiful, weeping Abilene – staring back. Even her tears are lovely, lovely enough to drink.

I turn away from the reflection, facing Abilene in all her glory. "I want to set you free, but I'm afraid of the brownie," I say sheepishly.

"There is no brownie. Your father made him up to scare you. If you spend all your time fretting over the brownie, then you'll never see who your father really is," Abilene says, her words hanging heavy as the rain clouds.

"Who is he?" I ask shakily.

"A monster. Just look at what he did to me for talking to you last week." She raises her arm, revealing an ugly bite from the blubber fork.

I shudder at the sight, pressing my ear to her ribs. "Your wound is singing. I can hear it!" I exclaim.

"Your wound is singing too."

"What wound?"

"Just listen," Abilene bids. She waves her hands over the water and a ribbon of light dances around her. Something is happening; I feel it moving through me as she circles her fingers around my heart.

But it's only the wind, sharp with my father's whistle. The sound cuts through me, turning me into a paper doll, frail and flimsy. I don't know whether I should believe Abilene or my father. But one thing is certain: I must be slick as a seabird if I'm to survive their twisted game.

# 21

## Abilene

I shut my weary eyes, my grief bone-deep, my body in knots I can't untie. A memory finds me in The Hutch, pinching a nerve inside me. I press my hand to my heart and feel my spirit rising, leaving behind muddy earth and moldy leaves.

When my eyes flutter open, I'm back in my oyster bed. A ray of light creeps through The Hall of Mirrors. My sisters are already awake; I hear them singing. I feel their dark little magic pulsing with mine.

Gran Opal usually slumbers beside us on a bed of cockleshells. To rest in her presence is the greatest honor, for she casts her dreams on us while we sleep. But last night was different; Gran Opal slipped away to Shimmer Cave. Ever since The Great Divide, she's been longing for The Jubilee.

The glorious day is finally here: Earie's fifteenth birthday. By the light of the moon, Earie will wear the hag stone around her neck and bind herself to The Deep Dark Nether.

I swim to The Hall of Mirrors as fast as I can. Peering into the gold-spun glass, I comb the sea tangles from my hair and paint my lips with a sea poppy. My sisters gather around me, tongues hissing, cheeks flushing, tails melding into one bright muscle.

"Any sign of Earie?" I ask.

“Not yet,” Florie swishes. The old eel swims beside her faithfully, his belly glowing with memories.

When Earie was a little mermaid, she slept with us in The Hall of Mirrors, but now she sleeps in The Octopus Lair among the mazes and the trenches. Every morning, she leaves before dawn to make it to The Hall of Mirrors in time for breakfast. Her skin blisters terribly in the sun, so we always give her the shadow seat as we float around the table.

But Earie isn’t here yet, and the sun is already climbing. We swim through the coral garden and peek through the pearl-edged shutters. Florie is the first to spot our queenfish. She cries out to Earie and waves her over, joy bubbling in her throat.

I catch a glimpse of Earie as she rounds the corner, a vision of brittle hair and vicious tentacles. She dances through the coral garden, parasol in hand to shield her from the harsh sun. She wriggles through the shutters, her violet eyes meeting mine. Earie hesitates to touch me, as she always does.

I know the price of hugging Earie, but she’s my queenfish, and I suffer her gladly. Squashing my fear, I wrap my arms around her. A sharp breath later, my wrist is on fire. I grit my teeth through the pain, venom coursing through my veins.

My sisters and I swim back to The Hall of Mirrors, Earie trailing behind us, dodging every shaft of light. As our eldest sister, Fairah has the honor of preparing Earie for The Jubilee. Fairah pats a pretty clamshell chair, but Earie's body isn't made for sitting. With a lopsided scowl, Earie swats her tentacles, forcing them to bend to her will. They bite her, the savage beasts, teething through her flesh.

Fairah stirs a giant pot and tosses in a pinch of sage, a handful of moon snails, and a sliver of bonefish. She charms the pot to a boil until a haze of smoke dances around the rim. With a ripe smile, she pours the steaming draught into a silver chalice, one of her many ship-wrecked treasures, and hands it to Earie. Eyes gleaming, Earie tips her head back and gulps the potion, then hisses in satisfaction.

The sea responds to the scent of dark little magic bubbling around us. Our eyes roll back in our skulls. Florie digs her fingernails into my flesh, painting the water fright-red with my blood. Orla pants with pleasure, arching her tailbone where skin and scales meet.

It's the dawning of a new day. Earie has never looked more beautiful; her reflection bounces off the gold-spun glass. She smiles, fangs bared against blood-red lips, her skin hanging from the bone. Earie twirls around, then plunges further into the deep. We follow her all the way to Shimmer Cave, tucked away in a shadowy trench, where all the brittle things sleep.

My heart hammers in my chest as we approach the entry; I crane my neck to get a better look. A cone of light reveals a sundry of creatures. Some are dressed in needles with eye stalks jutting from their skulls. Others have see-through skin and haunted hearts. Earie stops just short of the entry, her tentacles hissing. We've waited centuries to see Shimmer Cave, so I nudge her to keep on swimming. Hot on her tail, we squeeze through the narrow opening.

The first thing I hear is the surge of whirlpools, joined by the rush of sea whips. Whales watch us from the peepholes outside, clicking in celebration. We pass through a rustle of seaweed swaying with the current. Overhead, swarms of jellyfish drift through the inky water.

Gran Opal greets us with a smile, wrapping her wrinkly tail around a sandstone pillar. Her amber eye summons Earie. My sisters and I wriggle onto a slab of limestone; we don't want to miss a single second. We can't even bear the thought of blinking, so we snag a few crabs and pry our eyes open with their claws.

We watch as Earie glides through the eelgrass and bows before Gran Opal. They embrace each other for a tender moment, then Gran Opal creeps to the deepest corner, void of any light, where the hag stone hides. She pulls it from the dark abyss and charms it with her tongue, licking and sculling. As she fastens the hag stone around Earie's neck, it falls perfectly between her breasts.

"The hag stone belongs to you, Earie, along with all its magic. See the hole in the center?"

Gran Opal points. “It’s a mouth and a belly; it’ll absorb your pain.”

Mesmerized, Earie rubs the hag stone, sliding her finger through the empty hole in the center, relishing its splintered edges. Her tentacles quake, and the sea bursts into song.

*Sing we angelfish on high.*
*Sing we of The Deep Dark Nether.*
*Sing our tongues of blood and sand.*
*Sing our bones eternal.*

Earie joins the chorus, her voice enchanting us. Our bodies soar, rising higher and higher, a carnival of sticky fins and sugary lips. We slide our tongues through the cracks in the ceiling, licking and hissing, reaching for the stars.

Our melody lingers long after night has fallen. Washed in moonlight, all is still and bright. Gran Opal leads us to a grand feast; piled high on a rock shelf are delicacies in every shape and color. Our bellies growl, and the sea echoes our hunger.

I gorge on a juicy lobster. Earie cracks open a sea urchin. Gran Opal pries an oyster from its shell and slurps it down. Florie and Orla share a giant squid, their lips black with ink. Fairah raises a chalice to her lips, savoring the tang of sea vines on her tongue. Praise be to the noble creatures who sacrificed themselves for The Jubilee.

By midnight, our guests are full to the gills. They worship Earie one last time before they swim back to their grottos and lairs. Even the goblin sharks, with their empty eyes and knife-sharp teeth, pay their respects to our sister.

When we're alone, just us sisters, Gran Opal flicks her tongue in satisfaction. "On this sacred occasion, we pledge ourselves to our queenfish. Though Earie has suffered much, she's honored her true nature. She's our bone-dancer and our salvation. Remember this moment, my precious angelfish. Etch it on your hearts; feel it beat inside you. If we want to inherit The Deep Dark Nether, we must protect our queenfish to the bitter end."

We thump our tails against the eelgrass. "We're willing to sacrifice ourselves for our queenfish," we chime in unison. "Better a few of us die than all of us lose The Deep Dark Nether."

"Fear not, my sisters," Earie reassures. "If you make it to The Deep Dark Nether, I'll sing your bones eternal. But if you must sacrifice yourself, it will not be in vain." Earie swims under a streak of light. Her voice is fierce as a river, the moon rolling down her shoulders, the stars slipping through her fingers. "One black and blessed night, I'll sing you into saints of the sea, and you'll roll with the tide for eternity."

# 22

## Senga

Abilene is fading, a wisp of ancient history, a shell washed away by the tide. As she slithers into The Tide Pools, I sit on the edge, dipping my toes in the chilly water. She floats beside me, forcing me to notice her dire condition.

Try as I might, I can't tear my eyes away from her tail, rash-red and wilting.

Abilene looks as though she's been holding her breath for a thousand years, all empty eyes and wan skin. Even the brittle starfish on her breasts are dying, crumbling like leaves in the dead of winter.

With parched lips, she draws a shaky breath and sings. Her song soars on the wings of the wind, her voice cutting me, drawing blood like thorns.

*Sing we angelfish on high.*
*Sing we of The Deep Dark Nether.*
*Sing our tongues of blood and sand.*
*Sing our bones eternal.*

The saltwater slowly brings Abilene back to life. Her eyes glow like stars in the sky. Her cheeks flush pink with melted sunrise. Oh, how I want to hold her in my arms, but I can't bring myself to do it. After all the pain my family has caused her, the least I can do is give her a moment of peace. As much as it hurts, I never want her to stop singing, and yet I'm relieved when she does.

Is this love? To be so close and yet so far? To want something that hurts and heals in equal measure? To hear holy bells ringing in a candlelit shrine?

But I know I'm not welcome in shrines, so I shiver outside in the cold among the hawthorns and fairies, listening to the sound of my heart breaking. I don't long for bells or gods or relics. I long for the people inside, holding hands, warming each other with their own little fires. I long to be part of something good, to sing a song I've never sung.

Abilene reads the emotion on my face. She peels me with her eyes, biting into me like an apple. I can't bear the silence, so I glide over to her and press a finger to her shoulder blade, tracing her shark-toothed scars. "I don't want my family to hurt you or your little fry," I breathe, my voice barely a whisper. "I've tried to intervene, but there's no stopping them. They believe Kilda is going to turn them into gods. I know I shouldn't, but I love my family, even though I hate the evil things they do." I gaze up at The Peekaboos, tears caught in my throat.

"You remind me of my sister, Earie. For centuries, she lived as though she was a flounder, weak and powerless. No matter how cruel Kilda was, Earie always wanted Kilda to love her, just as you want your family to love you. It's natural to love your family." Abilene touches my cheek tenderly. "It's hard to be born in the darkness, always searching for the light, but you can escape the darkness whenever you're ready."

"How?"

"Become the light," Abilene croons.

I love the salt of her hiss, the way it rolls off her lips. "I want to be the light," I say, goosebumps prickling on my skin.

"My time is waning, angelfish. The Feast of the Singing Wound is upon us. My little fry will be here any day, and after she's born, your father will take her away from me. Please, set us free before it's too late."

"But if I set you free, my family will hate me."

Abilene looks up at the ragged sky, a pinch of scared and a heap of disappointed. "Why should you keep your family while I lose mine? After all, it's your family who wants to kill me and my little fry." She bites out the words, rubbing her belly.

I imagine her little fry with icy eyes and tiny fingers. I feel so guilty for what my family has done to them, for what *I've* done to them. Abilene forces a smile, but it's a thin disguise. I know she's crying on the inside, just like my mother. I've left my mark on them. I see it staring back at me, dark circles rimming their eyes, accusing me of things I never meant to do.

A wave of affection washes over me, tender words spilling from my lips, words I've never spoken before. "I love you, Abilene."

"I love you too, angelfish." She charms the water with her fingers, playing it like a harp. Up from the deep, a silver-spun mirror floats just out of my reach. Abilene preens in the looking glass, then she dangles it in front of my face. I scry the mirror as hard as I can, but my reflection is nowhere to be found. There's only Abilene, beautiful Abilene, with hungry eyes and hollow cheeks.

# 23

## Senga

Tonight's the night. Come hell or high water, I'm setting Abilene free. I can't bear her savage screams any longer. I know what I must do: kill the brownie and steal the key to The Hutch. I know just how to do it, too. I'll bash his skull in with a rock so he can't hurt Abilene anymore.

The brownie is here; I feel his slimy tongue between my thighs. I clap a hand over my mouth to keep from screaming. I steady myself and slip out of bed, dropping to my knees on the earth-worn floor. I reach under the bed and grab the rock.

The brownie yelps and flees, as if he senses my intentions. After swatting the cobwebs from my face, I light a candle until it hisses. I tiptoe outside, the flame burning low, wax dripping down my fingers. I cover the candle quickly with a glass chimney.

The hawthorn tree calls out to me, its branches swaying in the wind. I lie down on the cursed ground, my heart in my throat. I wait for the brownie, but he's nowhere to be found.

I doze off, snapping awake in fright. The sun rises from the belly of the earth, kissing me with its warmth. There's no point in waiting on the brownie any longer. I must set Abilene free before my father wakes. I'll have to make do without the key.

I claw at the freshly spit mud, chubby worms flying overhead. I dig deeper, sweat beading on my neck. My fingers nick something hard and cold. Much to my surprise, it's not The Hutch but a gnarled root, soaked in Kilda's dark little magic. Her foul blood reeks of poison and I nearly gag. I dig around the root frantically, tilling the ground until my nails are bloody nubs, but there's no sign of The Hutch.

Footsteps echo through The Blackhouse, followed by my father's loud snort.

My heart sinks. "I'm so sorry, Abilene," I cry, my tears soaking the ground. I quickly cover the hole and smooth it over as best I can.

# 24

## Abilene

Bound by the ghost rope, pain spikes through me. My body feels like something from a nightmare, as though a whale has beached himself on me. My hands are pinned beneath my spine, knees smashed against my belly. I haven't caught a deep breath since last Friday at The Tide Pools. The Hutch is caked in excrement, and the stench is unbearable. Oh, how I long to plunge into the deep salt sea and sway with the eelgrass.

My little fry beats on my belly like a caged bird singing of sky and water. Against all odds, she's still alive, but she's a prisoner inside me and she may never taste freedom. My voice is a scratch of nothing; I can't even sing her to sleep. Death laps against us like waves. I'm so afraid. If we die before dawn, I want her to have my mother's name.

"Thora," I murmur with cracked lips. I'm desperate for a moment of comfort, no matter how fleeting, so I close my eyes and conjure a memory.

After The Jubilee when Earie was of age, my sisters and I swam with her to Crescent Isle. Gran Opal said she was finally ready to sunbathe on The Crooked Sands. We'd never been on land before, and we'd never seen such a beautiful sight.

A blade of light pierced the fog, brightening the beach. Our hearts hammered as we wandered through a graveyard of shriveled starfish and icy driftwood. We slithered further, scraping our bellies on the black sand, until we found a sapphire pool. We took turns swirling our arms through the frigid water, catching bonefish with our bare hands.

When our bellies were full, we lolled on the shore while ghost crabs skittered across our tails. Sunbathing left me pink and tender, but it was excruciating for Earie. She wilted like a sunburnt flower, her tentacles screeching, dying a golden death. An urge seized me as I watched her suffer. I grabbed Earie's parasol and tried to shield her, but Gran Opal swatted it away.

"Earie must burn on her fifteenth birthday; it's written in the skin of the sea," Gran Opal hissed, flicking her tongue at me. "Earie was born in the dark, and she must become the light. I know how much it hurts to become the light, but Earie must embrace her pain with a willing heart. It's the only path to The Deep Dark Nether." Gran Opal slithered closer, wrapping her wrinkled tail around me. "You're our mirror-keeper, Abilene. You must encourage your sister. You must remind her of her true nature."

I took a deep breath and waved my fingers, conjuring a silver-spun mirror from thin air. "I know it hurts terribly," I whispered, lifting the mirror to Earie's blistered face, "but you must remember who you are. We need you, Earie. You're our queenfish, and you must honor your true nature. You're a black pearl from The Bitter Sea, and your pain will set us free."

Earie mustered a smile through bared fangs and welcomed the pain. I counted the seconds until sunset, stroking her hair and wiping the sweat from her brow. Finally, the cruel sun sputtered out, bruising the sky deep purple.

On the fringes of twilight, a mighty ship pushed through the waves. I propped myself up on my elbows and craned my neck to get a better look. A red flag flapped in the wind, bearing the name *Carnage*.

In a flash, Gran Opal scrambled through the shallows and swam hard for The Cauldron, Orla following hot on her tail. I cast Earie a worried glance as she laid corpse-quiet on the sand, her eyes glittering with tears.

Fairah, Florie, and I swam to a giant rock where the water was neck-deep. We hoisted ourselves onto it and sprawled out under the silver moon. We made conversation, a few human words here and there, but mostly swishes and hisses. We placed bets on who would win the annual dolphin races. Naturally, I bet on my beloved Zale.

As the ship came closer, the stink of mutiny filled the air: fermented flesh and blood-stained sails. When Gran Opal caught a whiff of it, she blew on her conch shell to warn us.

Earie roused at the noise, shaking the seaweed from her hair.

"Sing to them, Earie! See if there are any souls aboard who remember their true nature!" Gran Opal cried.

With a faithful nod, Earie parted her lips and sang. We joined the chorus, our voices trilling with the sea.

*Sing we angelfish on high.*
*Sing we of The Deep Dark Nether.*
*Sing our tongues of blood and sand.*
*Sing our bones eternal.*

A sudden clap of thunder shook us, followed by the sound of hissing sparks. Our instincts warned us to retreat; with stiff spines and goosebumps, we threw ourselves from the rock and plunged into the sea.

Gran Opal and Orla stirred The Cauldron, whipping the waves into a vicious whirlpool. With a flick of their wrists, a monstrous wave battered the ship, knocking a drove of men overboard. Petrified, they wrestled with each other, but there was one soul among them who remembered his true nature, and he cried out for us to save him.

In a mad splash, Earie surfed the stormy sea and rescued the scrawny man. He clung to her, cutting himself on her brittle hair, blood gushing from his hands. They shared a ragged breath under the gloaming, then Earie swaddled him in sailcloth and carried him to The Deep Dark Nether.

In the calm after the storm, I gazed up at the rust-red moon, my pulse finding a steady beat. Gran Opal lifted her conch shell once more, curling her lips around its pink edges. She blew, then she plunged underwater. We followed her all the way to The Deep Dark Nether. We darted past hungry goblin sharks and wiggled through trenches and mazes. We followed the scent of Earie's dark little magic, growing stronger with every league.

The current turned on us without warning, sending our bodies reeling. When it finally spit us out, we found ourselves in a giant cavern with mountains of bones and bodies in all states of decay. Some were still fresh, with bright eyes and pure hearts; others were cut to ribbons, rotten flesh hanging from the bone.

This was the moment we'd been waiting for – the chance to see The Deep Dark Nether with our own eyes.

Earie emerged from the shadows, her violet eyes glowing. As she rubbed the hag stone around her neck, we heard a strange clatter. It was the rattle of bones, beautiful bones, dancing all around us: skulls and femurs, tailbones, twisted spines, and heartless rib cages.

Before we could catch our breath, Earie roped us with her tentacles and took us to a wall of shelves bursting with jars of all shapes and sizes. There was a voice inside each one, waiting to be reunited with its body. Earie grabbed a tall, skinny jar and pressed it to my ear. At once, I felt a rush of dark little magic, not *my* dark little magic, but a stranger's. For a moment, I slipped into his skin and bones. I felt a pair of strapping human shoulders and horns on my head. I even felt his joy and his pain flowing through my veins.

My sisters and I spent hours pressing jars to our ears. When we hooked our tails together, we heard all the jars singing at once, a chorus of dark little magic swimming through us. Though the voices were different, they were one and the same: the same spirit of suffering and of salvation.

But I'm falling away. I feel the memory slipping through my fingers, a wonderfully sore memory that has bruised my heart. I'm not a little mermaid anymore, pressing jars to my ears. I'm a frightened mother with a child in my belly. I reach for my tail, but it's gone. I'm stiff with legs and land.

It's half past midnight; the moon tells me so with cold specks of light. I watch as they filter through a hole in the ground. I long to escape, but I don't dare move a muscle. The Hutch is a cruel contraption, lined with shards of glass waiting to spear my belly.

# 25

## Senga

It's a dreadful day for trekking to The Tide Pools, but Abilene needs to soak in the saltwater. She's too weak to walk; when she tries, her knees buckle.

"We can't have the sea hag dying on us before The Feast of the Singing Wound," my father grumbles. "Kilda expects a sacrifice, and that's exactly what I'm going to bring her." My father grabs Abilene by the waist and hoists her onto Ash's back. She whimpers sorely as he ties her down with the ghost rope. She shoots me a desperate look, her rosy hair threadbare.

A storm is coming. The clouds hang heavy; the air is a wet rag, slowly drowning me. I burrow into my wool cape, trying to escape the bitter cold. When I look up, there's nothing but a wall of grey and the sound of seagulls crying, warning us to turn around.

Each time Ash slips on the blade-sharp cliffs, my father whips him. Try as I might, I can't steady my own feet, either. One false move could send me over the edge, tumbling towards a rocky death. The thought grows on me. A broken neck can't be any worse than how I feel right now. Anything is better than having to watch my family sacrifice Abilene and her little fry on Sunday.

After the treacherous descent, my father heads north to fish. Though I can't see the ghost rope that binds her, Abilene insists it's there. I tug at the invisible knots until they break loose, cursing under my breath. She tumbles into my arms with a startled hiss. Her body creaks as we slog through the black sand. When we reach The Tide Pools, she slithers into the saltwater, nursing the bald patch on her scalp.

Glumly, I slip into the water, angling away from her. I don't want to see her monstrous body. I don't want to witness the misery I've caused her. I rub my breastbone, soothing my shattered heart, where the pain is sharp as glass.

"You're in a horrid mood," Abilene remarks. Despite her grave condition, she tries to cheer me, dipping underwater and tickling my feet. With a splash, she breaks the surface, her lips grazing my knees. I try to force a smile, but I can't bring myself to do it. As she floats beside me, I rest my head on her belly, listening to her little fry's heartbeat: *pitter-patter, pitter-patter*.

"Why are you so sullen, angelfish?"

"This morning my father told me the brownie isn't real," I say wistfully. "You were right all along. My father is the one who slays mermaids, but I don't want to follow in his footsteps. I don't want to be anything like him. I want to prove to *everyone* that I'm not a wicked bluebeard."

"*Everyone* is up there." Abilene raises a finger, pointing at the sea cliffs. "But I'm right here. Do you understand?"

I shrug my shoulders, feeling lost.

Abilene swims closer and takes me by the hand. "You can't be the light for everyone, but you can be the light for me and my little fry. Both our families have done cruel things to each other. After all, it was my sister who poisoned your isle. But we can be the light for each other, Senga. If we can see each other for who we truly are, apart from our families, then we can conquer the darkness together."

The fog rolls in like something from a dream, but I'm wide awake. I feel every inch of my body, every groove, every ridge, every valley. I feel my breath flowing, my feet planted in the sand.

A song rings through the air, unbroken and beautiful. I press an ear to Abilene's chest, tracing the source of the sound. She pulls away with a tender look, tears filling her eyes.

Awareness dawns on me; the sound is coming from me. *My wounds are singing.* I feel them churning inside my chest. I see it all so clearly now: the bright armor of courage. I grab onto it, wear it like a second skin, feel it breathing down my neck. I make a promise to the wind and the stars, waving my hands through the air. I *will* save Abilene, come hell or high water.

I scoop her up and dash through the black sand, carrying her to the deep salt sea. Abilene melts into me, and we share a heartbeat, gliding as one creature. When we reach the shore, I bend over, sucking for breath. "You're free," I whisper. As I peel us apart, I can't tell where my skin stops and her scales start.

Abilene smiles at me, her bony hand finding my cheek. "From the moment I saw you, I knew you'd be the light for me. I knew you were a black pearl from The Bitter Sea."

Our eyes lock. Then the sweetest surprise: her lips against mine. I want to stay here forever, my mouth dropping like an anchor, the salt of her kiss on my tongue.

The sea roars and we break apart. With a flick of her wrist, Abilene conjures a silver-spun mirror and holds it in front of me. I scry the looking glass harder than ever before, searching for my true nature.

The air stills and my eyes flutter. Something wondrous is happening. Curious sensations swim through me: the tickle of gills and the swish of bubbles. My legs melt into a puddle, and a muscly tail appears in their place, tapering down my waist. I feel the thrill of the needle and thread, the divinity of stitching myself back together.

Before I can utter a word, Abilene drenches the mirror underwater. It disappears, along with my tail. She tucks a loose curl behind my ear, her hand trembling with dark little magic. "I must escape before it's too late. But I want you to know there's a place for you in The Deep Dark Nether. You'll always have a home with me and my sisters. If you call on Earie, she'll sing your bones eternal," Abilene promises.

A wave breaks against my waist, nearly knocking me over. Abilene steadies me, then flicks her tail and slips beneath the water. I watch as she fins for Crescent Isle. With each heartbeat, she gets smaller. I slog through the shallows, swallowing the lump in my throat.

A voice rages in the wet dark. “Senga Thistle!”

I whip around, nearly rubbing noses with my father. My blood runs cold, and my vision blurs, black around the edges.

“What in Kilda’s name are you doing? Stop the sea hag at once! If she escapes, it’ll be the end of us!”

“I tried to stop her, but she got away from me.”

“Don’t lie to me,” my father shouts. “She could barely stand an hour ago. There’s no way she could’ve made it to the shore without your help.” He yanks me by the arm, nearly popping it out of its socket. I twist free, yelping like a wounded animal. “I should’ve tossed you over the sea cliffs when you were born,” he snarls.

“I wish you did,” I hiss.

I wait for him to say something, *anything*, but all he can do is glare at me. With a snort, he hitches a wave and chases after Abilene. He swims scary fast, as though Kilda has given him a pair of wings. My eyes follow him until he disappears, along with the pale sun.

I drop to my knees, tears caught in my throat. Familiar feelings visit me; I’m slippery and faraway. As I turn to leave the water’s edge, I hear panting and splashing. I whirl around. An angry wave spits my father out, but he’s not alone. He has Abilene by the hair, dragging her through the foam-kissed sand.

"Father, please, let her go!" I beg.

He raises his blade, cutting her to ribbons. Her blood spills ripe-red, sending a shiver through me as it drips from his hands.

Despite her mortal wounds, Abilene still fights for the sake of her little fry. She wrestles with my father, burying his head in the wet sand. She smashes him with her swollen belly, holding him down and suffocating him. My father kicks wildly, desperate for air.

Is blood thicker than water? My heart bleats like a lamb on the altar. A part of me wants to save my father, but my feet are pinned to the sand.

Abilene looks as fierce as she did at The Mooring: jaws cracked open, spine curved like a rainbow. She fangs my father's neck until he goes limp in her arms, then she drags him out to sea. As I stand on the lonely shore, the wind carries her song to me.

*Sing we angelfish on high.*
*Sing we of The Deep Dark Nether.*
*Sing our tongues of blood and sand.*
*Sing our bones eternal.*

# 26

## Senga

Supper is ready, but I'm not hungry. I ease into my chair at the table, rubbing the sore shoulder my father gave me. Gunn sits across from me, eyeing my breasts and draining the mead from his silver horn. I know exactly what he wants: to kill me and eat me all at once. I angle away from him, only to find my father's empty seat. As cruel as my father was, The Blackhouse isn't the same without him. I blink, biting back tears.

Lorna flounces into the kitchen, smoothing out a wrinkle in her dress. She never lifts a finger to help my mother cook, but she's always ready to reap the rewards. Lorna leans over my shoulder and sloshes a bowl of stew in front of me.

"I can't possibly eat," I groan.

Lorna huffs, clanging her spoon on the table. "I won't have you starving like a common landie. Lamb stew is too good to waste, no matter the circumstances. Your father's death was a terrible accident, but it can't be undone," she says dryly, taking her ruby locket in hand and polishing it on her neckline.

"It was no accident," Gunn cuts in. "How could you betray your own father, Senga? After everything he did for you! He could've tossed you over the sea cliffs when you were born with that disgusting caul on your head, but he let you live. I knew you'd be the death of him," he seethes, pounding his fists on the table.

"Gunn, please," Lorna whispers, stroking his hand.

He jerks away from her, sending the teapot to the floor with a shatter. "Did you even try to help your father, or did you just let the sea hag drown him?"

"I was scared. I didn't know what to do," I whimper, tears spilling.

"Your father is the one who kept me sane. Without him, I'm trapped in a house of she-devils!" Gunn shouts, on the verge of pulling his hair out. "Just look at the lot of you: a heathen, a nitwit, and a wife with a grave for a belly. No children to call my own and no son to leave my legacy."

His words land like a slap across Lorna's face. She stares at the soot-stained walls, wiping a tear from her cheek.

Gunn lunges at me, pouncing on the table. "You have no idea what you've done! Kilda is hungry, and our hands are empty!"

I shrink away from him, but he grabs my jaw and twists me closer. He lowers his voice to a whisper. "I pray a curse be on you, Senga. I pray Kilda burns you to the ground."

I tremble, a chill slithering down my spine. "We can go to Crescent Isle tonight and catch another sea hag. I'll do whatever it takes. I won't stop until I set things right," I vow, desperate to appease him.

Lorna rolls her eyes at me. "It doesn't work that way, Senga. We're only allowed to hunt during the thunder moon, and Kilda will only accept the first mermaid we capture each summer."

"If there are rules, why didn't someone tell me?" I yell, my cheeks burning red.

"Because we're your elders, and we don't owe you explanations," Gunn bites back. "If you had obeyed your father like you were supposed to, none of this would've happened."

Lorna glances at my mother. "You know what this means, don't you?"

My mother rocks back and forth, cradling her chin in her hands.

"What does it mean?" I cry.

"Kilda is coming for you," Gunn taunts.

My mother pads over to me and squeezes my hand. "Don't be afraid, little thistle. I'll be the sacrifice," she soothes, her voice ringing clear as a bell.

"*Your voice – it's beautiful*," I sputter, choking the words out. I feel faint, as though the rug has been pulled out from under me. The room spins, ashes and stars all around me. Pain jolts through me, the happy kind found in freshly stitched wounds. "Please, don't leave me, mother. I don't want you to be the sacrifice. There must be another way."

Gunn scowls at me. "There's no other way. Someone is going to The Brittle Forest, and you can bet it won't be me. It's you, or your mother," Gunn snorts, picking a scrap of lamb from his teeth, as though he couldn't care less.

"I'll go at dawn," my mother says softly.

Half past candletime, my mother cradles me in her arms. I hear Gunn and Lorna through the walls, rolling around in bed, begging Kilda to have mercy on them.

My mother tilts my chin, holding me with her gaze. She struggles to speak, her voice creaking like a trunk full of buried treasure. "You've dreamt of the needle and thread, haven't you?"

"Yes," I gasp. "I've dreamt of stitching my legs together. How did you know?"

She rubs my legs and smiles. "Because I sent the dream to you. I loved a mermaid once, and she loved me."

"Are mermaids good creatures?"

"Yes," she rasps, her voice deserting her.

Sleep tugs at my eyelids, but I don't want the moment to end. It feels so good to have my mother's arms around me, rocking together like waves in the sea. She smells of sugar and cinnamon and memories from long ago, long before she had me.

By dawn's early light, my mother is gone. I mourn in bed all day, grey light streaming through the window. My thoughts carry me down shadowy holes, holes that make me wonder if my mother ever existed. Perhaps she was nothing more than a sweet dream with the voice of an angel.

At dusk, I untangle myself from the tear-stained sheets and light a candle. A dark shape flutters by, catching my eye. I rush to the window and fling it open. The raven caws and fans his feathers, trying to cheer me. I pat him on the head and pluck the message from his beak.

*You're never alone, Senga. I'm always with you.*

My lips bloom into a smile. Perhaps my grandfather is watching out for me after all. I picture his black eyes and his peculiar whiskers. I shake the grief from my bones and creep outside for some fresh air.

I follow the worn path to the hawthorn tree and lie down beneath it. I gaze up at the stars, crushing my skirts in my hands. I try to hold onto the peace inside me, but I feel it slipping through my fingers.

I may have set Abilene free, but I forsook my mother. I hug my knees to my chest, wishing that life was simpler. No matter where I turn, there's pain around every corner. In saving someone I loved, I killed my own mother. It should be *my* body smoking in The Brittle Forest.

I rub the rosette around my neck, pressing the black pearl into the hollow of my throat. What I wouldn't give to feel Ivor's arms around me, but there are too many secrets between us. He would despise me if he knew what I did to my mother.

The wind comforts me, thick with Abilene's song. For a fleeting breath, I'm tempted to do as she said and call on Earie in The Deep Dark Nether. The raven caws again, bringing me back to my senses, and I clap a hand over my mouth, stifling the urge.

# 27

# Earie

I killed my mother on the night I was born, or rather my wretched tentacles did. They snuffed her out like a candle so I would know her by smoke and never by flame. Gran Opal says it wasn't my fault; just as hungry souls come into the world, it was written in the skin of the sea long before I was born.

*The queenfish will wear a veil of tentacles, and she must suffer her venom gladly.*

If Kilda had it her way, I would've died with my mother, but Kilda doesn't have the power to kill me. What she does have, though, is an obsession with torturing me.

When I was a little mermaid, I prayed to Kilda because she was a god and I thought I needed her. I prepared offerings, burning my fingers to the quick, begging the wind to carry the sweet smoke to her. I thought that if I could earn her love, she'd stop tormenting me, but the more I begged, the more she took from me.

At every turn, Kilda tempted me to forsake my true nature. She accused me of killing my mother. She taunted my hideous appearance. She told me that Gran Opal was a liar and that my sisters didn't love me. She made a covenant with the bluebeards to hunt my sisters during The Mooring every summer. Kilda's appetite was insatiable; she even stole my true love away, bound her to a bluebeard, and trapped her in The Brittle Forest.

But Twila is always with me; her song is etched on my heart with needle and thread.

I'm not like the other mermaids. I don't explore the glories of sunken ships or dance under the stars with strapping mermen. I don't sleep with my sisters in The Hall of Mirrors, where the water is crystal-clear and dawn breaks angel-bright. While my sisters dream in their oyster beds, I sleep in The Octopus Lair, surrounded by stonefish and goblin sharks.

My appearance is dreadful, all candle bones and tangled tentacles. I'm a blurry apparition, terrifying to even the bravest of creatures. When I look in the mirror, a monster stares back at me: loose skin and crooked spine, hair spilling black as ink.

On many a lonesome night, I roll over and find the old eel beside me. Memories shine like fireflies in his belly. He's been following me around ever since Florie died. I love him and hate him in equal measure.

I arch my back as he ribbons his way inside me. Tail quivering, I wait for the pain to spark. I know it's coming; memories always hurt at first. Then it happens, fast as a bolt of lightning or a crack of thunder. The old eel presses on my wound and a scream pours from my lungs. I squeeze the hag stone around my neck, thinking of Twila.

Suddenly, the lair smells of cinnamon and brew, sand and fire. For a fleeting moment, I see her face through a ring of blue, staring back at me. But I know it's not real; it's only the old eel poking me with pleasure. Lost in the tickle of his tail, I imagine Twila's fingers witching for water inside me, rubbing me in all the right places. I hiss and claw at the rocks, spiraling into a blessed release.

As the old eel dives deeper, another memory bubbles to the surface: my fifteenth birthday.

Gran Opal said I must burn on my fifteenth birthday. When the time came, my sisters and I rose above the salt to sunbathe on The Crooked Sands. Gran Opal warned me it would hurt, but the pain was far worse than I ever imagined. Each time a ray of light peeked through the clouds, I writhed in agony. When the sun finally sank into the sea, I felt like a pufferfish ready to pop, skin oozing blood-red, eyes hanging from their sockets.

My sisters weren't accustomed to the sun either, but none of them burned as badly as I did. I saw the worry in their eyes when they looked at me, but Gran Opal told them I must embrace my pain with a willing heart.

*And so I did.*

While my sisters slept, I swam to Hourglass Isle, leaving a trail of tears behind me. Each move cut like a knife, but I kept my eyes on the northern sea caves. I'd heard about the healing powers of the wulvers, and I needed them now more than ever.

By the time I reached Wulver Cove, my lungs rattled and my tail shook like a leaf. With a clumsy flop, I planted my sore face in the sand. I let out a yowl, and the pain yowled back, as though it was my oldest friend. Hoping for a miracle, I rubbed the hag stone between my fingers, but all I felt was a noose around my neck and a riverbed of blisters.

I rolled onto my back, a shipwrecked sight, flayed and ugly as ever. I'd greatly underestimated my strength. I could barely sit up, let alone crawl half a mile to the sea caves. I moped under the cold light of the moon, feeling like a fool.

I was half-asleep when something skittered across my tail. With drowsy hands, I swatted it away. A moment later, I felt it again. I jerked upright, searching for the source of my irritation. A smile tugged on my lips when I saw a ghost crab staring back at me, and I realized he wasn't an irritation, but an omen. Gran Opal taught me long ago that ghost crabs are the fortune tellers of the sea.

I cupped him in my hands, admiring his eyestalks and pincers. I rather liked his bizarre appearance. As I leaned in to get a better look, I heard his teeth rattling in his belly. It sounded like Gran Opal when she was fast asleep.

*Snap!* He pinched my nose. I yanked free and tossed him on the sand. Despite the sting, it was a good omen to be pinched. I could only hope it meant the wulvers were on their way to aid me.

I craved the solace of sleep, but I felt a song stirring on the tip of my tongue, begging for release. With a groan, I parted my lips and sang, but something was different this time. I heard another voice fusing with mine, the voice of a fallen angel. It was the loveliest sound I'd ever heard: bells ringing and bones breaking. I peered into the gloaming, desperate to find the source of such marvel. I feared she was a dream, a wish too wonderful, a puff of nothing.

Her song grew louder still. Oh, how I loved the lonesome edge of it, like an arrow piercing my heart. I spun towards the sea caves, and there she was, in all her glory, lips pursed, still singing – but she wasn't the feathered angel I'd imagined.

Torchlight warmed her face, revealing human features. Never had I heard a voice so divine or seen a woman so beautiful. I watched her from the corner of my eye as she loosened the hood of her cape. She smiled at me as her mahogany hair danced in the wind. One look at her, and I knew she was earth and stone and withering roses. She was everything I'd always wanted to be.

She took a step towards me, her demeanor pure and true. But her amber eyes startled me, the familiar shade reminding me of Gran Opal. A ragged breath seized me, and I feared I was in grave danger. Nothing was what it seemed on Hourglass Isle. Humans were dangerous, and I didn't know if I could trust her.

Perhaps this woman was a pawn in Kilda's game, sent to torture me. It was the only explanation; a sensible woman who saw me by torchlight would either run away or spear me. And yet here she was, this angel-eyed woman kneeling beside me.

I urged my body to fin for the sea, but I was utterly exhausted. The thought of swimming back to Crescent Isle was unbearable, so I steadied myself with a cleansing breath and waited. I pined for her touch more than anything, even more than The Deep Dark Nether. "Do you come in the name of Kilda?" I asked.

"I come in the name of Goldie," she answered. "My father is Lord Goldie. We live in the castle above the sea caves." She pointed at the sandstone bluffs.

I looked up, craning my neck.

"I suppose you don't care much about lords and castles," she said awkwardly, toying with her sleeves. "You don't have to be afraid."

"I was taught to fear all humans."

"You're wise to be wary, but I'm not like most humans. My father has instructed me well. I know all about the eternals, so you don't have to worry. I mean you no harm. I just want to help you."

"Why do you want to help me?"

She scooted closer. "Because I wish to serve you, Earie."

"How do you know my name?" I hissed, my lungs heavy with land and sky.

"The wulvers told me about you a long time ago. I've learned a great deal from them, including their remedies. I'm here to help ease your pain."

"I'm sure you're familiar with land creatures, but do you really know how to heal sea creatures?" I asked skeptically.

She nodded, smiling with such mirth. "Last winter, I healed a selkie. A squall threw her against the rocks and nearly split her in two. I stitched her flippers back together and concocted a salve to banish her pain. The summer before, I nursed a kelpie back to health after his mother was speared to death, and I've mended the broken wings of many sea birds." An emotion flickered on her face; perhaps it was embarrassment. "Forgive me for blathering on. I should've introduced myself properly. I'm Twila Goldie, the lady of Wulver Cove." She paused, her cheeks blushing. "Truth be told, I'm a little flustered. I didn't expect you to be so lovely."

"Please don't lie to me," I whispered.

"You don't believe in your own beauty?"

"I'm no fool. I'm hideous."

"I know you're miserably burned, but you'll heal in time."

"The burns may heal, but my face will always be dreadful. I was born like this, an ugly lopsided candle with wretched tentacles."

"If your face is a candle, all the better. Bless those who burn, for they bring us light," Twila said brightly, tilting my chin. Her amber eyes blazed into mine, the dark of night dipped in golden sun.

I dug my elbows into the sand, resisting the urge to move closer. I wrestled with my tentacles, begging them to behave, but no matter how hard I tried, I couldn't stop them from coiling and hissing.

Twila leaned into me bravely, her lips vibrating with song. Her voice was the rawest magic I'd ever known.

"You mustn't touch me. They'll sting you," I warned.

"I'm not afraid of your stubborn tentacles," she soothed, deepening her gaze. "I have immunity; I can put them to sleep if you let me."

Something in her eyes made me surrender – something warm and tender. I stayed bone-still as she massaged my tentacles. For the first time in my life, rather than putting up a fight, they fell into a deep sleep. Twila squeezed each one, releasing just enough venom to give me relief. I dropped my head forward, a blissful murmur escaping my lips. Nothing had ever felt so good. My head tipped like a teapot, the sorrow spilling out of me.

"It feels divine," I gasped.

"I'm just getting started," Twila smiled. She rooted around in her satchel. With a halting breath, she cracked open a jar of strange-smelling salve. The earthy aroma tickled my nose, all mint and grass. Behind closed eyes, I relished her soft hands all over me, turning me slippery inside and out. I felt the warmth of her voice humming inside me as she pulled a ribbon of light through my ears.

At last, I was light as a feather, all skin and bones and beating heart, all swan neck and soft belly. What was this feeling? Was it peace? Was it rapture? How could I tell? I'd never felt this way before.

Twila gently broke off her song and traced her fingers around my heart. "Your teeth are chattering, and your ribs are a sheet of ice," she whispered. "A wee fire and some spiced brew will do you a world of good."

I sat up, wrapping myself in my arms as a shiver tore through me. "I never realized how cold it was above the salt. A fire sounds grand, if it's not too much trouble."

"No trouble at all," Twila said, rising to her feet, setting out to warm me. She chipped and rubbed, stones giving way to sparks. When the fire bloomed, she hung a copper pot over the flames. Mesmerized, I watched as the water rolled to a boil. When the sweet concoction was ready, she filled a mug and handed it to me. "Here, have a nip of spiced brew."

I took a long sip, savoring every drop. Nothing had ever smelled so divine or tasted so delicious, bursting with cinnamon and cherries. It was a far cry from the stench of rotten seaweed in The Octopus Lair.

Twila sat down beside me, her velvety hair grazing my shoulder. "How did you come by those violet eyes? I've never seen anything quite like them."

"They were a gift from my Gran Opal. A consolation prize since the rest of me is so ugly. They're just like my mother's."

"Tell me about her."

"My mother died the day I was born. I never really knew her."

Twila cast her sad eyes on me. "I never knew my mother either, at least not in flesh and blood. But once upon her ghost, I loved her. When I was a child, I visited her in the turret of the castle and baked her soul cakes on her birthday and made merry with her on Christmas and Hogmanay."

All through the night, and many nights after, Twila held me on the edge of the sea caves. She braided my hair as I closed my eyes and listened to the seals barking in the kelp beds. Twila did all the touching for us, wrapping her legs around my tail and her arms around my waist. She pressed her tongue against my neck, licking away my pain. I wanted to touch her more than anything, to wear her soft skin against mine like the silk dresses my sisters found on sunken ships, but I couldn't bring myself to do it.

Twila was a thing of wonder, an angel so beautiful that I didn't dare touch her. I worshipped her from afar instead, head bowed and fingers clasped. I prayed to the ridge of her collarbone, to the smile lines on her heart-shaped face, to her succulent lips, all honey and nectar. I prayed for her to love me in the cold breath of dawn before the world wakes.

But I feel her fading away, the memory curling like smoke, rising to a heaven I'll never know. When I touch the slit below my navel, it's empty. The old eel is gone, my oyster bed soaked in tears. If not for the old memory-eater, what would become of Twila? Perhaps I'd only know her as a wrinkle on my cheek. A twitch in my eye. A scratch in my throat. What the mind forgets, the body remembers with vengeance.

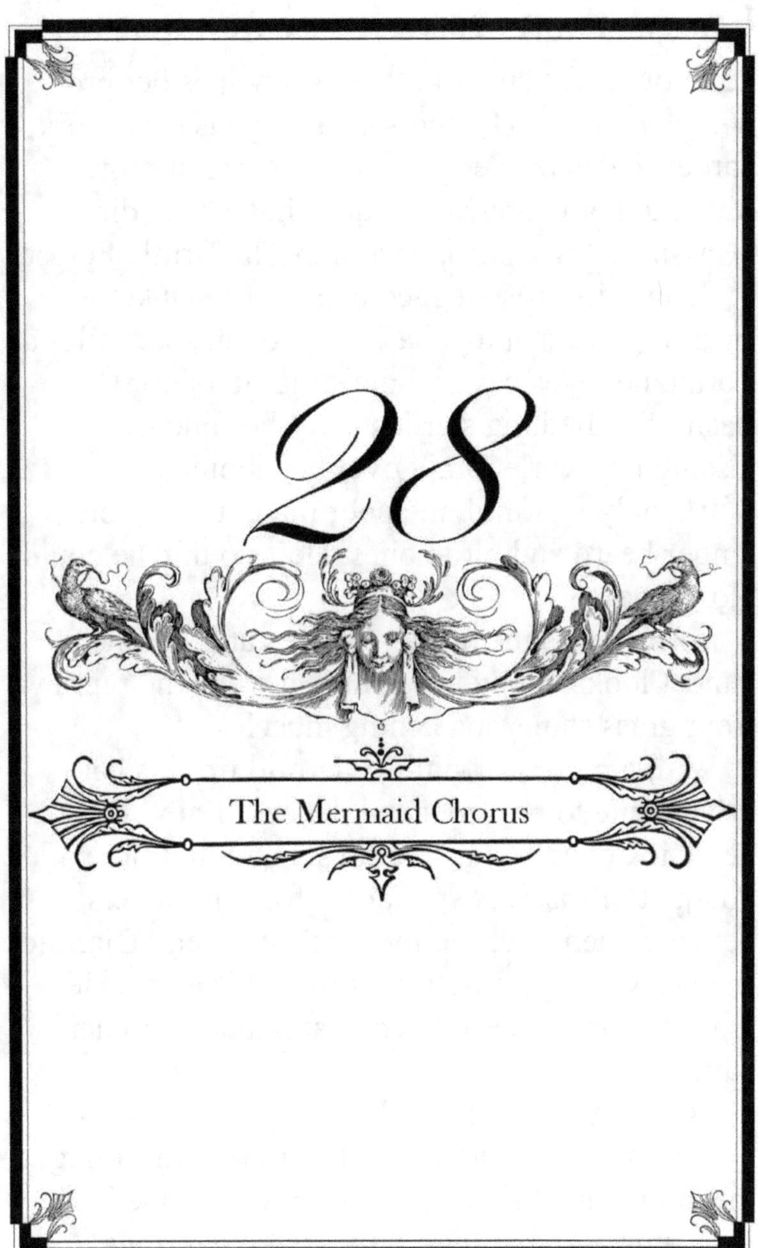

# 28

## The Mermaid Chorus

Under the yolk of the sun, Lorna sweats through her blouse. Cursing out loud, she wipes her brow with her sleeve. Hoeing for cabbage is hard work, harder than she ever gave her sister credit for. Much to her dismay, her hands have been dirty ever since Twila disappeared in The Brittle Forest.

Senga sits cross-legged on a wool blanket, snapping beans into a basket. Though she smiles at Lorna, her eyes have all the sting of a jellyfish. A flash of something startles her. She flinches, tossing her scarlet braid over her shoulder.

It's only Diarmid, the poor man, nothing but ginger beard and bird bones. He's so thin he could blow away.

Lorna drops the hoe and waves at him. She almost looks happy to see him, a welcome reprieve from grass stains and aching muscles.

With a mournful smile, Diarmid tips his hat. "I've come to pay my condolences. Truly, I'm heartsick over Twila," he says, handing Lorna a bouquet of roses. A spark of affection flickers between them, but it only lasts a moment. Diarmid snags a white rose before Lorna pulls away. He crouches down beside Senga and tucks it in her hair.

"Thank you," Senga whispers.

Diarmid rises and looks at Lorna. "I'm sailing to the mainland at first light. I should've done it a long time ago. It's high time someone brings justice to Hourglass Isle."

Lorna pulls a clump of mud from her hair, whimpering in disgust. "Justice? Whatever for?"

"For all the cloven women I've seen wash up on your shore," Diarmid says, tightening his jaw.

"Cloven women?" Lorna scoffs. "That's preposterous. Your hunger has clouded your judgment. Come inside and have a nip of brew."

"We just made dessert," Senga pipes up.

"Dessert, you say?" Diarmid grins, his eyes wide with curiosity, the kind that kills cats.

Diarmid follows their swishing skirts into the kitchen. The walls are sooty as ever, but the lampblack hardly matters compared to the cloying sweetness of sugar, bread, and berries. "It smells divine," he swoons, his belly growling. "Where should I sit? I wouldn't want to provoke the brownie."

A smile tugs on Lorna's lips. "You can sit wherever you like. We've no need for the brownie anymore. Our little thistle is all grown up, as you can see."

"Indeed. She's the shine on the apple," Diarmid praises, plumping a cushion at the head of the table.

Lorna sits beside him. "About these cloven women," she says, batting her lashes. "It must be the work of a shark or some brutal sea creature. Trekking to the mainland will only be a waste of energy. You'll create a stir, and it'll lead to nothing. It'll damage your reputation. You must think of Sorcha and your children. What if they need you while you're gone? What if *I* need you?" Lorna says sweetly, patting his knee.

He raises a playful brow. "You haven't needed me in ages."

Lorna tries to persuade him again. "It's a terrible time to travel. Snowfall is coming; I can smell it."

Diarmid chuckles, waving a hand at her. "It's too early for snowfall. I'll take my chances."

Lorna rolls her eyes and takes a sip of tea. "Suit yourself, but don't say I didn't warn you. I can see the snow clouds out the window."

"Lorna," he whispers, his hand circling her wrist. "I know there's more to the story than you're telling me. I find it hard to believe that Twila and Warr drowned. Maybe they had a quarrel? Maybe things got out of hand? Maybe Gunn killed them both in a fit of rage?" Diarmid studies her intently, searching for clues, but her face could trick even the keenest of hunters. "I've seen cloven bodies more than once. For all I know, Twila could've met a similar end. Things have gone too far. Next time, it could be you, or, heaven forbid, Senga."

"Warr and Twila drowned! It was a terrible accident; there's nothing more to tell!" Lorna shouts, jumping to her feet. She flicks her eyes at Senga. "Don't just stand there like a bump on a log. Tell Diarmid what you saw. You saw your father drown, didn't you?"

Senga nods obediently.

"And what about your mother?" Diarmid asks.

“Leave Senga alone,” Lorna cuts in. “Let her grieve in peace. She’s been through enough already.”

“And so have you, my love. What a pity, losing your only sister.”

Lorna softens her voice. “Are you sure I can’t convince you to stay on Hourglass Isle?”

Diarmid polishes a spoon with his sleeve, considering the matter. “I’m afraid not. I’ll be out with the tide tomorrow morning.”

“Then we’ve no time to waste,” Lorna says, whirling on her heels. She prepares the sweet bread, sprinkling it with spices. She plucks a bowl from the cupboard and fills it to the brim. “Fancy a taste of my raspberry buns?”

Diarmid grins, his belly growling. “I thought you’d never ask.”

Lorna flicks a runaway raspberry at him. He catches it nimbly and eats it. Laughter fills her throat as she sets the bowl down in front of him. “Eat up,” she purrs, her voice soft as cream.

Diarmid slices the bun down the middle. He nearly inhales the first half, licking his sticky fingers. “You should sail to the mainland with me tomorrow. Gunn is a man to be feared. We can testify against him.” He pauses to finish the last half, then washes it down with a swig of brew.

“Gunn isn’t the one you should fear.”

“Are you mad? Of course he is.”

“Gunn didn’t lace your berries with wolfsbane. *I did*,” Lorna sneers.

Diarmid blinks in shock, wiping his lips with the back of his hand.

The fire dims, along with Lorna. She's darker than ever before, her face a forest of shadows. "Did you really think I would let you meddle with Kilda's dark little magic after everything I've sacrificed? Mark my words, I'll become a god if it's the last thing I do. No one can stop me, especially not *you*."

Diarmid chokes, grabbing frantically at his throat. He drops to the floor with a thud, his breath shattering, his face splotchy blue. He foams at the mouth like a wild beast, his lips smeared with berries.

Senga falls to her knees, fumbling with his body. She turns him on his belly and thumps between his shoulder blades, desperate to pound the poison out. She shoves her hands into his mouth, pulling the muck out of him. "No, no, no, please, don't go," she sobs.

But it's too late; the damage is already done. His eyes roll white as he slips beyond the veil.

Senga draws a shaky breath and kisses his forehead. She plucks the rose from her hair and lays it on his chest. She trembles to her feet, wiping her slimy hands on her skirt. Something white-hot burns inside her, urging her to destroy Lorna, to grab her by the neck and break her collarbone. To crush her windpipe and strangle the life from her lungs.

Their eyes lock for a moment, but neither of them move a muscle.

Senga tries to scream, but her voice is little more than a whisper. "How could you do that to him? He *loved* you."

Lorna lifts her chin, sharpening her tongue. "To love is to die, so you'd better stay away from that filthy wulver, unless you want to dig him an early grave."

"I don't love Ivor," Senga lies.

"Good, because love makes you weak." Lorna bends over, looking down at Diarmid. With a groan, she drags his body across the floor to the front door. "I told him snow was coming," she gloats.

The door slams shut behind her, sending a gust of icy wind through The Blackhouse. Senga dashes to the window and peers outside, where snow is falling like scraps of lace. She shudders, pulling her cape tighter, unshed tears stinging her eyes.

# 29

# Senga

Lorna carries on as though nothing has happened. She soaks in milk baths and brightens her hair with tallow. She primps at her dressing table, wetting a cloth with rose oil and dabbing it behind her ears. But I know she's not alright; I hear her wounds singing late at night, rattling her tiny black heart.

Early this morning, I baked soul cakes for Diarmid and my mother. Even now at high noon, the air is still pumpkin-sweet. Lorna leads the way to the hawthorn tree as I trail behind her. She snaps her fingers, prodding me to hurry. When we reach the dreadful spot behind the twisted trunk, she crouches down, her eyes sharp on me. I squat down beside her, obeying her command as I grab Diarmid's legs.

We drag him through a field of faded heather, where my mother and I used to pick fairy bells on sunbaked days. I sidestep a rabbit hole, nearly twisting my ankle. I try not to look at Diarmid, but he's staring right at me, his eyes frozen wide, his tongue hanging out. His skin is a troubling shade of blue, all icy moon and muddy veins. He reminds me of the seal I found last summer, stiff and bloated and stinking with rot. I bury my nose in my sleeve, taking only the shallowest breaths.

With a groan, Lorna halts just short of the sea cliffs and wipes the sweat from her brow. "I can't take another step. We'll burn him here."

I look at the harp-shaped hills to the west where a flock of sheep are grazing. The moment they spot us, they stop and stare, big-eyed and long-tongued, fearing the worst. Lorna drops to her knees and arranges Diarmid's body beside a tumble of stones. She rustles in the grass, striking her flint until it sparks. I squeeze my eyes shut, wishing I was anywhere in the world but here. I swim in the darkness behind my lids, counting the minutes as they slowly pass.

A gust of heat smothers me with vengeance. I crack an eye open only to find Diarmid's body fading to black, crumbling in the flames. I bow my head, biting my lip until it's bloody. Here burns the Constable of Hourglass Isle, a man I loved, in my own way. A man who was kinder to me than my own father.

Lorna stands silently, waving her hands through his ashes. She clears her throat, nearly growling, willing her heart not to break. Suddenly, she rips the ruby locket from her neck and feeds it to the flames.

I frown. "I thought grandfather gave you that locket."

"No. Diarmid gave me the locket when he asked me to marry him," she says wistfully. "I didn't want Gunn to know because he would've destroyed it, so I lied and said it was from my father." Lorna looks down at the sad remains, a wisp of hair veiling her damp eyes. "Diarmid, my darling, you're the only man I've ever loved," she confesses. After a mournful breath, she turns to me and whispers, "I couldn't let him leave this world without hearing me say it."

Words escape me; I don't know what to say or feel. I've never seen Lorna like this before, on the edge of tears, refusing to slip over. "If Diarmid is the only man you ever loved, does that mean you don't love Gunn?"

"Of course I don't love Gunn," she snaps. "What's to love about a drunken oaf? He would've had *you* in our bed by now if you'd shown him a lick of interest."

My belly roils, heat crawling up my throat. "Why did you marry Gunn if you didn't love him?"

"Because he brought me to Kilda. When I called on her, milk and honey rained down from the sky, and she promised me I'd be more than a footprint washed away by the tide. Kilda taught me to stop loving men and start loving myself. As hard as it was, I had to let go of everything I ever loved, but that's what it takes to become a god," Lorna declares, planting a palm between her breasts. "You'd be wise to learn from me, little thistle. Love is every bit as poisonous as wolfsbane; it's a truth as old as time. To love is to die."

"But what if Kilda is the poison?" I whisper. "What if we're not that different from the sea hags and the wulvers? What if we've forgotten our true nature?" I hold my breath, half-expecting her to dip me in jam and feast on my stupidity.

Lorna lifts her chin and sharpens her tongue. “There’s no such thing as true nature, only the stories we tell ourselves. Kilda is *my* story. Do you really want to take that away from me? Just think of all the pain you’ve caused our family, and yet I’ve let you stay in The Blackhouse. You really should be more grateful, Senga.” Suddenly, a petrel chatters above us, filling the air with its musk. “Listen to that,” Lorna coos. “Kilda sent us one of her petrels.”

I couldn’t care less about Kilda or her petrels, but I don’t dare tell Lorna, lest I find my tea laced with wolfsbane tomorrow morning. “Do you think my mother loved me?”

“She died for you, didn’t she?”

A chill slides down my tailbone.

Lorna smooths her hand over my cheek, softening her expression. “When your father wanted to slay you, your mother hid you in the sea caves. When Kilda was hungry for you, your mother smoked herself into a burnt offering. She burned so you wouldn’t have to. That’s how much she loved you.”

Lorna holds me with her gaze, her eyes flickering. A strange emotion sparks between us, flame-gold and ash-warm. A part of me wants to throw myself in her arms and hug her, but I don’t trust her. She’s as clever as a rook and every bit as sneaky.

# 30

## Ivor

The Teahouse is full of whispers; even the ghosts are talking about *the string of mysterious disappearances*. First, it was Warr, then Twila, and now Diarmid.

"People don't just vanish into thin air, *do they*?" little Aila whispers, her eyes wide with fear.

Sir Craig chuckles. "Not unless they're ghosts."

Sir Quinn cuts in. "I bet a pot of gold that Gunn and Lorna are responsible for the disappearances." He crunches on a biscuit stale enough to crack his teeth.

Lady Graham swallows the last of her brandy. "I know you'll think me soft as jam, but I almost feel bad for Senga. The poor thing lost her mother and her father, and now she's all alone with Gunn and Lorna. I hate to think she might be next."

"If Senga disappears, I say good riddance," bareback Bonnie huffs, planting her fists on her hips. "Why should I feel bad for her? She's never lifted a finger to help any of us."

"Hear, hear," Sir Craig cheers.

My grip tightens on the table as I bite back my anger. I hate the way they talk about Senga. I've tried to put in a good word for her, but all they see when they look at her is a well-fed, well-dressed heathen. With a wolfish smile, I stand tall and take my leave. Senga has been on my mind all week. I would've already checked on her and paid my condolences if it weren't for Mina's fragile condition. But I can't delay the visit any longer, not when people are disappearing, and Senga's life could be in danger.

It's a dreadful night for trekking to The Blackhouse, but the urge to see Senga is stronger than ever. Broon wanted to come with me, but my bones needed a good stretch. I drop down on all fours, dead leaves crunching beneath me. I rear my head back and howl, fur prickling down my spine. I dash over the hills and through the glen. An owl hoots in the treetops, matching the wild beat of my heart. Fog wreaths around me, the sky grey as smoke.

A smudge of light captures my attention. I spot Senga just outside The Blackhouse, bent over the wash basin, shaking the cinders from her hair. I stand upright, shaking the wild from my bones and wiping the mud from my hands. I don't want to startle her; it's half past candletime, and she's not expecting me.

"Senga, it's me," I whisper.

"Ivor?" she whispers back, stepping closer. "What are you doing here? You shouldn't be out in the cold."

My mouth is a river, pent-up words breaking free. "I had to see you tonight. I had to make sure you were alright. I'm so sorry about your mother and your father. Are Gunn and Lorna inside?"

"No, they're in The Brittle Forest, swigging mead and mushroom hunting."

"Diarmid and I looked for you in The Brittle Forest last month. We thought your family might make a sacrifice to Kilda, but we couldn't find you."

Senga looks away, smoothing her fingers through her damp hair. "We didn't go this year because of what happened to my mother and father."

I swallow hard. "I heard they drowned. Is it true?"

Silence hangs between us like a noose, her lips grave-tight.

"Have you seen Diarmid lately?" I try instead.

"A few weeks ago."

"Well, he seems to have disappeared. Sorcha said the last time that she saw him, he was on his way to pay his condolences to you and Lorna. Did something happen when he visited? Did he and Gunn have a scuffle?"

Senga looks up at me, her eyes shining like emerald tarns. "I can't tell the truth, and I don't want to lie to you, so please stop asking me questions."

My gaze lingers on her heart-shaped face. She's positively luscious, soft in all the right places, her plum-red lips begging to be kissed. "I think you should leave The Blackhouse tonight. Let me help you, Senga. You can stay with me and Mina."

"If I stay with you and Mina, then you'll both be in danger."

"I'm a grown man. I'm not afraid of your uncle," I say gruffly.

"Well, you should be. You must leave, Ivor. It's not safe for you here."

Edgy, she leans into me, a snag of thorns and petals. She smells of roses and raindrops and memories that never happened. I sweep my palm over the apple of her cheek.

"Will I see you at the teahouse on Hogmanay?"

"Lorna and Gunn will never agree to it."

"If I don't see you there, then I'll send you the raven."

Her body stills in shock. "The raven?" she breathes. "You mean *you're* the one who's been sending me the raven all these years? I thought it was my grandfather."

"Well, it *was* your grandfather's raven, but the poor creature fled the castle when it went up in flames. I thought he was long gone, but then he came to my window one stormy night, and he's been with me ever since." I pause, tucking a damp curl behind her ear. "If you ever need me, call on the raven."

Senga musters a smile, tightening the ribbon at her throat. "I will, but you better go home before it gets any colder." She lingers for a moment, looking like a wrapped present in her snow-white cape. Before I can open her, she turns on her heels and casts her candle into the darkness.

I watch until she disappears inside The Blackhouse. As I follow the stony path through the glen, my imagination runs wild. I picture Senga slipping out of her gown, brushing her flame-red hair by the fire. She lays down, wearing nothing but bedsheets and rose oil, her fingers creeping up her thighs, exploring her secret garden. She hisses until her throat is raw, the delicious sounds filling my ears, sounds I long to evoke. But longing is a cruel god, stiff and unforgiving, and in a blink, the croft appears.

I wish I could sleep outside, alone with my desire, but Mina needs me. I close my eyes and listen to my father's wisdom rustling in the leaves.

*The only treasure you keep is what you bury in your heart*.

I bury Senga in my heart, covering her with dirt and flowers. All through the night, I feel her settling under my rib cage, my chest a freshly dug grave.

# 31

## Senga

Hogmanay comes and goes. The landies celebrate without me, singing merrily and sipping sweet cherry brandy. Visions of Ivor and Mina dance through my head while I sulk at the spinning wheel. Kilda's altar is my only companion. High above the hearth, lamb bones and rowan branches glare at me through tendrils of smoke.

I pass the long winter making dolls as my mother once did. This is the way I want to remember her, with a spool of silver thread and a thimble on my finger. She made the most beautiful dolls, lovely enough for royal children. Dolls with big brown eyes, salt-white stockings, and tiny slippers.

I cradle a fresh doll in my palm, sewing a handful of chestnut hair through the crown of her skull. As I glide my fingers over the cold porcelain, I study her blank little face. What expression suits her? Which colors and textures? I hear a faint murmur: birds and flowers. I dip a brush in the paint and swirl it around, dabbing the excess against a cockleshell. I tint her cheeks petal-pink and her eyes robin-blue. After she dries, I wrap her in sunny silk and a white sash.

*She looks happy.* The kind of happy I've always wanted to be. She makes it look so easy.

Perhaps a new dress would make me happy. There's a bolt of jade silk that would be perfect for my freckled skin, but I resist the temptation, turning my attention to Lorna instead. If I want to survive, I must keep her happy, and nothing brings her more joy than a new dress. When she slips it on, it's as though she still lives in the castle. Many mornings, I find her spinning in front of the gilded mirror with a smile on her face and her train in her hand.

Lorna has tried to be patient with me. As for Gunn, he holds a grudge, even though I break my back sweeping and harvesting, spinning wool, chopping wood, and tending to the sheep and the ponies. Nothing I do is ever enough, and I know he'll never forgive me.

Grief is a flightless bird, a bony creature chewing time the way flames eat wood. Day turns to night, trees crumble to ashes. Winter fades and spring melts into summer, each day like the one before until a glimmer of hope finds me.

Tonight, the rose moon blooms, marking the summer solstice, and tomorrow great fires will burn in its honor. I've waited all winter to share my dolls with the landies. I hope to make a friend, though I know my chances are slim.

A soft breeze blows through the window as I lie in bed, tangled up in the sheets. Caught in a restless net, I squirm in the half-light of dreams as a waterspout spins around me. I feel the poke of the needle, the pull of the thread. I feel the squeeze of tentacles dragging me under. Even as I'm drowning, I try to stitch my legs into a tail.

As I float through the graveyard of dreams, a voice screams beneath each stone. Some just need a friend. Others long to rise like flowers and feel the sun on their skin. Some are angry and want revenge, like my father. I feel him in this place, all hooves and harp strings, unraveling me at the seams.

I jolt awake to a flutter, a pitter-patter against the glass. Deep in the candlelit shadows, the raven appears. I pad over to him and creak the window open. He fixes his dreary eyes on me and flaps his wings wildly. I pat him on the head, plucking the damp message from his beak. It crackles as I open it, rough and sweet with Ivor's voice.

*Come to the summer solstice and watch the fires burn with me.*

Ivor still thinks of me. I'm as happy as the doll I painted, all silk and sash and pink cheeks. I try to fall back asleep, but I'm full of wingbeats and tingles between my thighs.

At the break of dawn, I roll out of bed, still damp with desire. I stand next to the low burning candles, cupping my naked breasts, thinking of Ivor. I want him to want me; I want him to notice all my curves and edges. I squeeze into my black corset and pull the ribbons tight, then I slip into a scalloped blouse that flatters my figure.

*Oh, the things we do for love and all its torturesome pleasures.*

I tiptoe past Gunn and Lorna's room, taking extra care not to wake them. Despite feeling queasy, I force myself to eat a small bowl of porridge. The moment I finish, I dash outside, wiping my mouth on the back of my hand.

At the wash basin, I'm a body in motion: scrubbing my face, brushing my teeth, combing and pinning my hair. After I'm done primping, I catch a glimpse of my reflection in the window: a long neck just waiting to be bitten. Lips dark and full as the moon. Blood-red curls piled on my head. I like what I see, and my breath hitches.

I blink and the morning is gone. The sun peeks through the clouds and finds me packing a basket of dolls and a jug of water. Ash nuzzles my arm as I ready him for the solstice. At noon, we ride down to The Teahouse. As we descend the harp-shaped hills, there's nothing but rainy slopes as far as the eye can see. We slip and slide through the mud, my thoughts drifting with the sound of his hoofbeats.

Suddenly, the fog breaks like a spell, giving way to the hustle and bustle of the world below. The landies shout at one another, smoking pipes and trading jokes. Sir Quinn sits behind a round table, peddling his latest treasures: handsome daggers and shields in every shape and color, hammers and nails for all the hard workers, and even a few candlesticks for those with delicate natures. My head swims with sounds: carts clicking on cobblestone, ropes creaking, sails whipping in the wind.

In no time at all, a bug-eyed woman spots me. If looks could kill, I'd be dead. She turns to the widow Lusk and gossips in her ear. I angle away from them, gently pulling the reins and nudging Ash with my leg. Thanks be that he's such an obedient creature. Right away, he trots over to a cluster of junipers. I make a quick dismount, planting my boots in the mud. Ash sighs, bracing himself for a long wait. After I tether him, I pat him on the rump and head for the harbour.

Broken vessels bob in the sea like ghosts longing for former glory. A gust of wind sweeps inland, reeking of low tide and sour armpits. Overhead, octopuses hang from a line, their tentacles baking in the soggy sun. A throng of drifters elbow past me, carving a path to The Teahouse. They don't know it yet, but they're about to be sorely disappointed, especially the one with a barrel for a belly. The Teahouse can hardly feed the landies, let alone drifters on the wind.

I spot an empty table outside The Teahouse, my pulse quickening as I rush to claim it. I set the basket down on the salt-washed wood and arrange the dolls carefully. When I finish, I take a step back, marveling at a winter's worth of hard work, but I'm not the only one admiring the grand display. A crow-haired girl dashes over, dragging her weary mother behind her.

"Please, mother, please, may I have a doll?" The girl begs, tilting her head sweetly.

Her mother scowls at me. "You know we can't afford a doll. Why else would you have brought them here but to torture our children?"

I kneel beside the girl and tuck a pretty doll in the crook of her arm. "It's a gift. I don't expect anything in return. I only meant to bring you a bit of joy," I smile.

The woman pecks the air with her nose. "If you really wanted to bring us joy, you would've brought milk and lamb. Dolls won't fill an empty belly, will they?"

"Please, let me have it!" the girl cries, clutching the doll tight.

Her mother snatches it away. "Absolutely not. I'm certain it's bewitched."

"Bewitched? Of course not," I stammer. "I was only trying to spread some cheer."

"You and your family have done nothing but cause trouble. You're not welcome here, Senga. Just ask anyone, and they'll tell you," the woman sneers, spitting the words at me. In a huff, she grabs the girl's scrawny arm and storms off.

The sun sinks, along with my heart, a cold shatter in the dark. I shove the dolls into the basket and light the lantern. I curse under my breath, looking positively mad as I trudge back to Ash. Everything annoys me: the sound of people laughing, the white masts piercing the sky, the smell of birds on moldy nests.

Ash nickers as I round the corner; at least he's glad to see me. "Let's go home," I whisper urgently. Just as I'm about to mount him, a pair of strong hands clutch my waist.

"Not so fast," Ivor coaxes. "Watch the fires burn with me." He plucks a doll from the basket, the very one I made in his image: a little boy in a black tunic, with eyes of melted gold. "What a handsome doll. He looks just like me," Ivor teases, his eyes crinkling at the corners. "I think I'll keep him."

"You might as well. I've got a basket full of dolls, and no one wants them," I pout. "You can save it for your son or your daughter. I'm sure you and Mina will have a wee bundle on the way soon enough."

Ivor looks away. "I highly doubt it. Mina took ill this spring, and she still hasn't recovered."

I bite my lip, shame bleeding through me. "I'm sorry, Ivor. I'm in a horrid mood. I shouldn't have come here."

"I'm glad you're here," he whispers, his face full of mischief. He looks just like he did when we were children chasing fairies through the glen. Ivor holds me with his gaze, his beard braided, his eyes gleaming in the black of night. Then he turns and runs away.

I follow him on a wing and a prayer, my heart thumping as we climb a steep hill. Below us, landies sing and waves crash. When we finally reach the top, Ivor sprawls out in the meadow. I slither beside him and watch the ink on his neck throbbing for air.

Ivor turns to me and smiles, sweat beading on his brow. He presses closer still, with a touch so faint a breath could steal it away. His dead eye lands on my mouth, sparks flickering between us.

I want to wear the heat in his eyes. Catch the light like a firefly. Drag my lips along the rough of his jaw. I want to feel the length of him inside me, breaking me open, until blood wets my thighs, and I'm spiraling with pleasure.

I steady myself with crushed fists, the grass biting into my palms. I wait for a stolen kiss, but it never comes. Instead, Ivor laces his fingers through mine, bridging the dark between us. All through the night, we watch the fires burn while the flames lick the sky.

# 32

## Senga

Summer flees and the sky turns grey, washing the earth in autumn rain. Leaves dance through the oak trees, their veins inking burnt gold.

Gunn is chopping angry; the axe in his hand tells me so. He stomps his hoof-feet in the mud, wielding the axe above his head. I cover my ears as he unleashes his fury. Gunn pounds the splitting block so hard the ground shakes beneath me. I cringe as he lunges at me, catching me by the waist.

"You escaped The Mooring this summer because Lorna convinced me to let you grieve your mother. But you won't escape The Feast of the Singing Wound next month. I'll see to it." He pulls me tighter, his thumbs grazing my breasts. His lips find my ear, his breath hot on my neck. "I know you fancy that filthy wulver. Lorna told me all about it," he snorts.

Though I despise Gunn with every bone in my body, I dare not run away. "I don't fancy Ivor," I lie. "He's just my friend. I need at least one friend on this isle."

"Friend or more, you mark my words, I'll turn him inside out with my bare hands if you don't come to The Feast of the Singing Wound with us next month." He pauses, all big teeth and horse tongue. "Give me your word, Senga. I need to hear you say it. Say you'll help us sacrifice the mermaid, or the wulver dies."

“Of course, I will,” I whisper, making my voice honey-sweet. “You’ve let me stay in The Blackhouse with you, and I’m so grateful.” I bat my eyes and kiss him on the cheek. It sickens me, but I know it’s the only way to appease him.

Just when I think might retch from the smell of him, he releases me. “Sometimes you really are a good girl, Senga Thistle,” he says, his mouth a shipwrecked smile. There’s an edge to his voice, blade on bone, tearing clean through me. I hold my breath with clenched fists, expecting the worst, but he goes back to chopping wood and I scurry away.

All day and night, I’m stuck with the smell of him: sour loins and rotten teeth. Heavens and stars, what I wouldn’t give to bathe in The Tide Pools, but a nasty storm has trapped me inside The Blackhouse. Gunn knew I’d run to the sea and wash him off me if he gave me the chance, so he summoned a squall to strand me. Rain slants against the windows, thunder cracking, mud splattering everywhere.

Half past candletime, I’m still awake, spinning wool into winter comforts. I hum loudly, trying to block out the sounds of the poor mermaid. She’s been crying in The Hutch since supper. Gunn and Lorna captured her two months ago, but they won’t let me see her, not after what happened with Abilene. I hope with all my heart it’s not the queenfish. No matter who she is, I want to set her free, but I don’t dare try, because Lorna and Gunn would make Ivor pay the price.

Lightning flashes bright, and a vision of Abilene cobbles to life. My heart is an altar of smoke and sky, her words swimming through me.

*There's a place for you in The Deep Dark Nether. You'll always have a home with me and my sisters. If you call on Earie, she'll sing your bones eternal.*

With closed eyes and clasped hands, I pray to Earie, deep down in my belly, where Gunn and Lorna can't hear.

# 33

## Earie

The old eel stalks me, popping out of rock beds and snapping his jaw. I try to ignore him, but he ribbons around me, his belly glowing with memories. He catches a whiff of my desire, the scent of black mold and barnacles. I'm hungry for Twila, and he knows it. He grins at me, all jagged teeth and underbite.

I shut my eyes as he slips inside, haunting me with a memory. It washes over me like a wave lapping against the shore, pulling me back in time.

Wulver Cove. The smell of hot springs. Thunder and lightning. Taking shelter in the sea caves. The magic of Twila's voice as she plucks her harp. As I gaze into her angel eyes, I see all my sharp edges: fangs, tentacles, candle bones, and coral antlers. I look the same as ever, but I feel something I've never felt before.

*Beautiful.*

Twila is so close, close enough that I can smell the cinnamon in her hair. She blooms like a rosebud inside me, waking new desires. I want to kiss her soft petals and taste her sweet nectar. I slither closer, my tail snaking between the rocks. I wait for her to embrace me as she has so many times before, but she holds back. I'm dying to touch her, to shower her with affection, but I don't feel worthy of her love.

Twila senses my emotions. She deepens her gaze, her amber eyes blazing. "I love you, Earie, pure and true. I even told my father about you."

“I love you, too, with all my heart,” I whisper.

“Then be the first to touch me,” she tempts. Her lips have all the shine of an apple begging to be kissed.

Pulse racing, I thread my fingers through her hair. She leans into me as I palm my way down her neck, my hands creeping like ivy, twining around her waist, halting just short of her hips.

“You’re getting closer,” Twila breathes, peeling off her blouse and unlacing her corset with her nimble fingers.

I can’t tear my eyes away from her salmon-pink nipples. My heart leaps into my throat. As my need grows, so does my courage. I press a kiss to her neck, nibbling and sucking. With clammy hands, I caress her breasts, drawing a whimper from her lips. Twila leans back, sliding out of her underskirts. She’s naked now, save a strip of white lace hiding the hollow between her thighs. My tail quakes as she strips off the lace, spreading herself open like a butterfly.

Spider-soft, I creep between her thighs, rubbing her silky web between my fingers. She arches her back, her nipples peaking. I linger as a shudder claims her body. If Twila enjoys my fingers so much, then I bet she’ll love my tongue; I always knew it was made for more than singing. In the space of a breath, I taste her, my tongue sculling softly on her pearl. She murmurs, her breath uneven, her lips caught between her teeth. Like a teapot, she rattles and steams until her muscles soften.

Twila wastes no time in pleasing me. She doesn't even pause to crumple in my arms and enjoy the shiver. Hungrily, she finds the slit below my navel. I close my eyes, clawing at the rocks, her clever fingers deep inside my shell. In the shimmering dark, she cracks me open like an oyster, bringing hiss after hiss from my desperate lips. I feel all the thrill of an electric eel zapping me, but none of the pain. Outside, the sky splits with thunder and lightning, and the air smells of pouring rain.

My tentacles wake, and for once they're not petulant. They coil around us, tickling us with waves of sheer joy. We whisper in each other's ears, our necks bruised with kisses. We fly to the edge of eternity, the ground shattering beneath us.

I roll over onto my belly, my breath still heavy. I sense now is the time to be quiet, but a question burns inside me. "Are you betrothed to one of the men on Hourglass Isle?"

Twila smiles through a fringe of dark lashes. "My father has spared me such a fate. He knows all about you, and he wants us to be happy. You're my queenfish, and I want you to take me to The Deep Dark Nether."

"You'd really give up living in a castle for a cavern filled with sharks and bones?"

"In a heartbeat," Twila whispers. She smooths a hand over my cheek, pricking her finger on a coral antler. Between a flinch and a smile, a drop of blood bubbles on her finger. I crane my neck and lick it away. Even her blood tastes divine, all cinnamon and sugar. "Besides, castles aren't for women. They're for pretty birds with clipped wings," Twila continues. "I don't wish for castles. I wish for true love, and I've found it in you, Earie. I belong under the salt with you and your sisters. I want you to take me to The Deep Dark Nether so we can roll with the tide and pulse with the sea forever," she says, her eyes gleaming.

I stroke her hand, casting her a worried glance. "But Twila, we don't know if I'll inherit The Deep Dark Nether. Gran Opal says there's danger ahead. What if I take you there and something bad happens? You'd be all alone for eternity, without me or your family."

"You'll inherit The Deep Dark Nether," she says brightly. "I've never been so sure of anything. But we can wait if that's what you want. You can take me there whenever you're ready." She smiles, caressing my tail.

I want Twila to be with me forever. I want to take her to The Deep Dark Nether. But I can't bear the thought of her becoming a pile of bones, a heartless rib cage, a specimen trapped in a jar. Twila is with me now, alive and well, and that's all that matters.

Or so I thought.

The old eel slides out of me, taking the memory with him. Memories are just moments frozen in time; they don't tell the whole story. I can't be sure how far I've come, or how close I am to the ending. I can only feel what the old eel sticks inside me. And when he leaves, I'm left with scars that won't heal – scars I love to touch but hate to feel.

# 34

## Senga

Lorna sent me to The Teahouse this afternoon. She doesn't want me to be there when she takes *the sea hag* to The Tide Pools. She still doesn't trust me, not after Abilene.

In the past, I would've been thrilled to clink mugs with the landies, but now I've given up all hope of befriending them. Instead, I spend my time downstairs in the apothecary among the herbs and tinctures. Lady Graham has taken a shine to me, but she's not interested in friendship, only in the jugs of milk I bring her, which she kindly shares with her patrons.

The apothecary is dimly lit. There aren't any torches to be found, only a shrine of candles and pesky cobwebs that stick to my boots. It smells of sage and rot, but I don't mind. There's a comfort in being sick that's hard to describe.

A young boy with a mean limp pokes his head out of his scarf. I wink at him, and his lips curve into a half-smile that doesn't quite reach his eyes.

Lady Mirren stands beside me, a quiet woman with seven children buried in the ground. She pats my shoulder gently, her face wrinkled with loss, then she clasps her hands together and waits for her tincture. After forty years of being a spinstress, her fingers must throb.

Lady Graham is the only one who knows what ails me: *a lonely heart*, she calls it. I know laudanum is a poor substitute for friends, but it's the only thing that slays my nightmares. In the drowsy dark, I dream of poisoning Mina with wolfsbane. I watch as she clutches her throat, choking for breath, just as Diarmid did.

*Poor Diarmid*. The eel-thin man won't leave me alone. Every night, he slips through the cracked roof and floats above my bed, his face a leather hide stretched to the bone, his eyes black as ink wells. I beg him to forgive me, but he won't. Instead, he grabs me by the throat, and I wake choking for air, the sheets soaked in sweat. My mother visits me, too, a panting fallow with an arrow through her heart, her body curling into smoke.

Lady Graham waves her hand in front of me, capturing my attention. She smiles roughly and passes me a discreet bottle. I bury it in my pocket like treasure, breathing a sigh of relief. Peace is just a pony ride home and a spoonful away, but first I must escape the men in The Teahouse. As I climb the creaky stairs, I catch a whiff of their smoldering lust.

Sure enough, a pair of drifters gawk at me from a corner table, arguing over who'll have me in the pleasure chamber with its flimsy curtain and scurry of mice. The winner struts over to me. I can tell he's from The Bright Sea. His beard gives him away, blonde as cornsilk.

"I've sailed to the edge of the world and back. I've seen cities burned to ash and gods swallowed by the sea, but in all my voyages, I've never seen such beauty."

I flick my braid over my shoulder, unimpressed. "Flattery won't get you anywhere on this isle."

"Is that so?"

I nod, flashing an icy smile.

"What's your name?"

"It's better you don't know. I'm the daughter of a wicked bluebeard, and you'd be wise to stay away from me."

He chuckles, pulling a pipe from his pocket. "Lucky for you, I'm not afraid of anything. Come to the pleasure chamber with me. I'll show you what you've been missing." With a single stride, he closes the space between us. His scent lingers: leather and long nights at sea.

I set my mouth in a firm line, resisting his advances. "If you're a fortune hunter looking for high society, you'll be sorely disappointed."

He lowers his voice to a whisper. "I've had my share of fortune, and I much prefer passion." He lights the pipe and presses it to my lips. I take a puff, and the air turns smoky-sweet. I try to blink away the satisfaction, but he sees it shining in my eyes. "It's maple from The Bright Sea. Have another drag," he offers, sweeping his hand under my chin. I puff again, the smoke rising from my mouth like a burnt offering. "I like a woman who can handle a mouthful," he toys, twisting a lock of my hair around his finger. "Come to the pleasure chamber with me. What do you say?"

I'm tempted to go with him because Ivor has already been in the pink with Mina, but I can't bring myself to do it. I love Ivor, and I think he loves me, too. But then again, what would I know of love? A spark that catches and burns out so quickly.

The tea bell chimes and Sorcha appears, her ragamuffin brood trailing behind her. Without so much as a goodbye to the handsome stranger beside me, I make a mad dash for the back door.

Sorcha catches me by the arm. "Can I have a word with you? It won't take long."

"I was just leaving. I really need to get back home."

"Have you seen Diarmid?" she presses. "I know he's fond of Lorna. Perhaps he's been staying with you? I won't be angry. I just want to know that he's alright," Sorcha says, searching me with her bloodshot eyes.

"I haven't seen him in a long time," I say, forcing myself to meet her gaze.

Her daughters stare at me, all sallow skin and dirt-spun dresses. As I sweep my eyes over them, I can't help but notice their brother isn't with them.

"Graham died this spring," Sorcha says faintly, answering the question on my tongue. "He slept on a pillow of pine needles for a fortnight, but it was no match for his fever. I wish Diarmid could've been there." She looks away, her voice cracking. "I'm so lonely without him."

My vision swims, blurry around the edges. The world is rain, tears, and poison. I didn't see it before, but I see it now. There are ghosts on this isle. Lords whose castles burned to the ground. Mothers torn from their daughters and smoked into burnt offerings. Fools poisoned with wolfsbane. Widows dying of broken hearts, and fatherless children starving for food and affection.

I whirl around and flee The Teahouse. Sorcha follows close on my heels. I mount Ash frantically, then push him to a gallop. The wind howls like a banshee, haunting me with guilt. My heart pounds as we race through the glen and over the hills. I nearly break open the laudanum, but I resist indulging for fear of spilling it.

Ash slows to a trot as we cross the clearing near The Blackhouse. I draw a deep breath, steadying myself. He carries me to the pony pen, and I quickly dismount.

After tethering him, I creep inside and go straight to bed. I pop the cork and soak my tongue in the bitter syrup. In no time at all, I feel a hearth burning inside me, warming me from the inside out. Stars slip through the cracked roof, spinning little ribbons of light around me. Ivor is there on the edge of my dreams, eyes dark as molasses, shoulders broad enough to shore up the sea. My body rises to meet him. We float together, swathed in fog.

Then a noise pecks at my ears, shaking me from my dreams. It's the raven rapping on the window; I see his dreary eyes and his short wing. I stumble over to him, my feet still asleep, and tug the slip of parchment from his beak.

*I need to talk to you. Meet me in the sea caves tomorrow at midnight.*

# 35

## Ivor

I wait for Senga in the sea caves, my heart pounding with the waves. I mumble under my breath, rehearsing how to break the news to her. I don't want to scare her off. She's already been through so much. In the end, I decide it's best to come right out and say it.

Nothing has changed inside the sea caves. They look the same as they did when I was a boy, with their domed ceiling and limestone spindles. As I breathe in the scent of hot springs and moss, I think of my father splayed on the rocks. I'm caught somewhere between happy and sad, but isn't that the nature of nostalgia? It always takes more than it gives.

Senga blows in on a gust of wind. I hear her footsteps echoing. A smile tugs on her lips as she peers around the corner. "You must have quite the news if you summoned me here at midnight." She skitters over the slick rocks and sits beside me. The torchlight plays on her heart-shaped face, her ivory skin dusted in gold. "Let me guess. You and Mina have a wee bundle on the way."

I look down, shaking my head.

"I know you've been in the pink with her. It's only natural, Ivor, and you deserve to be happy."

I swallow hard, clenching my jaw. "Mina departed this world last month. She took care of me when I was a boy, and I'll always be grateful for her. May she rest in peace."

A long silence stretches between us. Senga casts me a worried look, crushing her skirts in her hands. “I seem to say the foulest things when I’m with you. I’m sorry, Ivor. Are you alright?”

“My conscience is clear. I paid my debt to the MacTacvish family, and I honored Mina to the grave.” I pause for a beat, fixing my eyes on her. “But I’m a free man now.”

Senga tucks a loose curl behind her ear. “Free to do what?”

“Free to speak my love for you after all these years.”

She gazes up at me, blushing. “Was I really betrothed to you when I was born?”

“Yes,” I whisper, lacing her fingers through mine. “And we can be together now, if you’ll have me.”

She bites back a smile, rubbing the chill from her shoulders. “Fancy a soak? It’ll keep the cold from settling in our bones.”

From the corner of my eye, I watch as she kicks off her boots and socks and slips out of her cape. With a devilish laugh, she peels off her blouse and wriggles out of her underskirts, tossing them into a crumpled pile. Words escape me; I’m nothing but a racing pulse.

“We may be betrothed, but we’re not married yet, so we should keep our necessaries on,” Senga says, relishing my tongue-tied surprise.

“Of course,” I utter, my heart falling through my rib cage.

Outside, gulls cry and waves pound the shore. But when Senga stands before me, nearly naked, pulling pins and ribbons from her hair, everything else melts away. She's a vision of beauty, exceeding even my wildest dreams. Pale flesh against ridges and valleys. Hair flaming red, curling down her shoulders. Breasts round and full as the moon.

She glides into the steamy pool, turning her back on me. After I undress, I slip in behind her, winding my arms around her waist. She faces me, soft and slow, our lips barely touching. My fingers climb higher, passing over her navel and ribs, snaking between her breasts, until I reach the rosette around her neck. I press the black pearl into the hollow of her throat. "Do you remember when I gave you this?"

"How could I forget?" she whispers. "It meant the world to me."

The air is needle-thin between us. Something is happening, something heady and feverish dominating our every breath. Senga feels it, too, and she surrenders. Her muscles soften as I pull her under. She floats freely in my arms, her scarlet hair bleeding in the water. I cradle her jaw in my hand, slanting my mouth against her plum-red lips. My kisses are soft at first, then harder as my hungry hands rove her body. I explore her tastes and textures: honeysuckle-sweet, the curve of her hips, the poke of her ribs, the slip of her tender parts.

All too soon, our lungs burn for air, forcing us to the surface. I reel in the water for a hazy moment, drinking in her beauty. She tilts her head back, her long lashes fluttering, wet whispers still on her lips.

I breathe into the silence before breaking it. "I want to help you, Senga. I know the feast for Kilda is coming and your family will make a sacrifice. I don't know exactly what it entails, but I'm sure it's something awful," I say, stroking her hair. "What does your family do in The Brittle Forest?"

Senga keeps quiet, the words locked so deep inside her they can't even reach her eyes, let alone her lips.

"If you tell me when your family is going, I can go to The Brittle Forest and try to stop them," I suggest.

Senga blanches, breaking away from me. "Let's not ruin a perfect moment by talking about my family."

"I know it's hard to talk about. I can only imagine how horrible it is living with Gunn and Lorna, but things are different now. We can get married."

Senga bites her lip, fear dancing in her eyes. "They'd never allow it."

"I could visit them tomorrow and ask for your hand in marriage. You could live with me in my croft, and they'd have The Blackhouse all to themselves. Perhaps they'd enjoy their privacy."

“No, Ivor! I don’t want you to come to The Blackhouse or The Brittle Forest! If you do, I’ll never speak to you again!” Senga cries, digging her nails into my wrists. She has all the trappings of a skittish creature: big eyes, sharp claws, and shallow breath.

“It’s alright, Senga. I won’t go to The Blackhouse or The Brittle Forest. I promise. I didn’t mean to upset you,” I say softly, pressing my palm to her shoulder. “We can leave Hourglass Isle if you want. We can sail north, past The Peekaboos, or wherever you want to go. I just want to be with you. That’s all I’ve ever wanted.”

“Me too,” she whispers, “but there’s something I need to do first.”

# 36

## Senga

I'm in the frosty meadow, lugging a pail full of blackberries, when the raven swoops down and perches on my shoulder. He caws and beats his wings against me, desperate to capture my attention. I pluck the message from his beak and smash it under my boot. He flinches, blinking his dreary eyes at me. It's the third time this month that I've sent him back to Ivor without a message. With an impatient flutter, he flies away.

I don't want to leave Ivor in the dark, but I can't encourage his affection. It's too dangerous. Gunn and Lorna might kill him just to spite me. And even if Ivor and I ran away, there would be no happy ending. Ivor fought honorably for his family, while I sentenced mine to death. His love for me is obscured by shadows; the Senga he loves isn't real.

I can still taste last night's laudanum on my tongue, soothing the ache in my lonely heart. The sky darkens without warning, soaking the earth in a cold rain. The air smells of fresh pine and bleak skies that never quite turn into snow. I pick up my pace, sprinting to The Blackhouse.

I'm tempted to stow away on a vessel in the shipyard, to leave everything behind, even Ivor. To find a place where no one knows me or my wicked family. I've given up on marriage, but I could eke out a living as a spinstress. I could start over and paint a new picture of myself. The notion is thrilling, filling my belly with wingbeats.

But I hear the poor mermaid wailing in The Hutch, and I know my conscience would never let me leave. Dread pulses through me. Tomorrow is The Feast of the Singing Wound, and I must go.

# 37

## Senga

We waste no time after mooring the lugger. The Feast of the Singing Wound is here, and Kilda is hungry. Lorna leads the way to The Brittle Forest, but first we must squeeze through The Wee Narrows, the thinnest passage on Hourglass Isle. When we reach the entrance, the landscape shifts dramatically. The sea disappears, and the sky collapses.

Inside the tunnel, it smells like death warmed over. I pinch my nose, stifling a gag. I stay on Lorna's heels, careful not to step on the hem of her dress. Gunn trails behind us, the mermaid slung over his shoulder like a sack of potatoes. She's too weak to put up a fight, and he knows it.

The further we go, the tighter it gets. The tunnel is smoldering hot, stealing the breath from my lungs. Beads of sweat pool between my breasts. Foul things lurk around every corner. One-eyed goblins spring from the clay, slashing my ankles with blade-sharp nails. Fallen fairies circle overhead, keen to lead me to one of their torture chambers. I plug my ears with my fingers, shutting out their screeches.

Just when I'm sure all is lost, a ray of light blinks in the distance. Instinctively, we make a run for it. We fall to our knees the moment we break free, shaking and gasping for air.

But the nightmare is far from over; the tunnel's scorching heat has given way to a frozen, wide-open sky. I wrap my cape around me, following

Lorna up a steep hill until we reach a lone rowan tree. Its branches blow in the icy wind, marking the entrance to The Brittle Forest.

Lorna bows before the rowan tree. “Kilda lives here,” she says in a sugary tone. “You must pay your respects, Senga.”

Feigning reverence, I bow my head and brush my fingers along the splintered bark. Gunn snorts loudly, making his presence known. I wince as he shoves the mermaid against the base of the trunk. She hisses and squirms, trying to break free. She looks up at me with ink-blue eyes, her lips a silent prayer. I never saw the ghost rope before, but I see it now, snaking around her, binding her to the rowan tree.

Gunn claps his hands in my face. “Don’t just stand there. Make yourself useful.”

Night falls and keeps on falling, chilling me to the bone. Dead leaves swirl through the air like snowflakes. I gather a bundle of twigs and branches for kindling, then strike the tinder again and again, breathing a sigh of relief when it finally sparks. I squat down, warming my hands by the fire. The wood melts into monsters with empty eyes and crooked noses.

I feel dazed, as though I’m in a trance. I hear the mermaid’s muffled cries as Gunn yanks her hair and gropes her tiny breasts, then he stabs the blubber fork clean through her chest. With a wild snort, he wields an axe over his shoulder, aiming for the top of her tail.

I will myself to rip the axe from his hands, but my body is frozen. Kilda's dark little magic moves sluggishly through my veins, all-consuming.

The axe hangs mid-air over Gunn's shoulder. He offers it to Lorna. "Would you like to do the honors?"

"I thought you'd never ask," Lorna beams, rushing to him. Without so much as a second thought, she snatches the axe and buries it in the mermaid. Lorna chops again and again, tearing off the tail.

Petrified, the mermaid watches her tail flopping beside her. Eyes bulging, she lets out a blood-curdling scream. It's the most feral sound I've heard, sharp enough to draw blood from my ears.

"Cut her tongue out, quick!" Gunn shouts, his hands over his ears.

Lorna closes her eyes, relishing the moment. "I happen to like the sound of pain." She kneels beside the mermaid, wearing a ruthless smile. She pulls a blade from her pocket and, with a brutal slash, cuts out the mermaid's tongue.

The mermaid's eyes roll back in her skull, her mouth a gaping hole. She can't scream anymore, so I scream for her, heat climbing up my throat. The world is red, gutted-red, everything blood and fire.

Then it dawns on me; I'm not screaming but gagging. I bend over, my tongue drenched in bile.

Gunn roars with laughter. "You better get used to the gore. You'll slay the mermaid next year," he grins.

I stare blankly at Lorna, my wits scattered by the violence. Lorna squeals with delight, spearing the mermaid's tongue on one of Kilda's branches. I hide my face in the crook of my arm as she spears the mermaid's tail. When she's done, she dances around the fire, her body curling with the flames. "Dance with me, little thistle," she calls.

I try to stand, but my legs are still stuck to the ground. Against my will, I lift my arms in the air, swaying back and forth. Snow falls lightly, dusting the trees. The flames rise higher, tickling my nostrils with the slow burn of pine.

Gunn plops down beside me and removes his boots for the first time. I catch a glimpse of his hairy hooves, lit by the fire. I shiver, clapping a hand over my mouth.

"What's wrong? Never seen a hoof as big as mine?" Gunn flashes a slobbery smile, filling his silver horn with mead.

When the fire fizzles out, Gunn takes Lorna by the hand. They creep over to a gnarled oak tree and lie underneath it. I make my bed in a large pine tree, far away from them. There's a hollow notch in the base of its trunk, perfect for protection. I squeeze into the notch, hiding from the icy wind.

Long after Lorna and Gunn fall asleep, I can still hear the mermaid's wounds singing; the dreadful sound hangs on a high note. I feel sick and thorny, sharp in soft places. I crawl through the underbrush until I find a spot to empty my guts. I wipe the sour taste from my lips and summon my courage.

Fallow Point is calling, and I must go. This very moment is why I came. The cold moon winks at me, a shard of glass in the cracked sky, lighting my way through the dark. I sneak to the rowan tree, careful not to wake Lorna and Gunn. I'm afraid the mermaid will be too heavy to carry, but I must try to return her to the sea.

After I tie her bloody tail around my waist and tuck her tongue in my pocket, I cradle her cloven body in my arms. It's much lighter than I expected, carrying someone in bits and pieces. My heart hammers as I scramble into The Brittle Forest. Petrels as black as coal try to chase after me, but they tumble to the forest floor, their wings broken.

I run with abandon, boots crunching through frozen leaves, teeth chattering like a music box. The trees blur, looking like scarecrows with sewn lips and straw hair. I shudder when I think of my mother dying all alone in these woods. Was it quick? Or did she suffer?

Chest heaving, I stop to catch my breath. Awareness dawns on me; there's blood all over me. I can smell it and taste it, and it's even worse than the gut baths Lorna gave me. "Mother, if you're here, please, help me," I beg, tears rolling down my cheeks.

Up ahead, I see a clearing. I dash towards it, tripping on a gnarled root. Instinctively, my hands fly in front of me to break my fall. The mermaid goes flying, her tail thudding beside me. I pick myself up and rub my aching wrists. As I retrieve the scattered mermaid, a herd of fallows approach from the east. They gather around me, clacking their antlers and stinking of rot.

"Mother? Are you here?" I scan the herd, searching for a sign, but there's no way to tell them apart. They all wear the same vacant expression, with the same bloodshot eyes and snow-white spots on their bodies.

As I settle back into my senses, I hear waves crashing down below.

*Waves*. My heart thumps. I take a careful step towards the sea, expecting the worst from the fallows. Much to my surprise, they break the circle, turning their attention to something beyond me. I watch them for a moment while they prance around a barren tree, looking sinister in the moonlight.

"Mother," I whisper. "If you can hear me, I'm sorry, and I love you." I choke the words out, wiping the muddy hair from my eyes. I wait a minute, but there's only silence. Though my heart wants to linger, my body urges me to leave the fallows behind. With each step I take, the waves get louder. I follow the sound all the way to Fallow Point.

Between heavy breaths, I call on the queenfish. "Earie, if you can hear me, please stitch this mermaid back together and show her the way to The Deep Dark Nether." I lean over the edge of the bluff, heaving the cloven mermaid into the salt below.

A gust of wind burns my frostbitten skin. Freezing rain pours from the sky, soaking my eyelashes shut. I long for candle-lit windows, a cup of hot tea, and Ivor's arms around me. As I turn on my heels, I hear the faint sound of singing wounds as the mermaid splashes into the sea.

# 38

## Ivor

I'm lost in dreams, so dark and sweet, when the raven raps on the window. The image of Senga fades, along with the thrill of being inside her. A strangled noise stirs in my throat, mid-pleasure. Tangled up in the sheets, I peel my eyes open. The room is washed in dull morning light, still grey from last night's storm. I drag myself out of bed, every inch of me aching for Senga.

Half-drunk on dreams, I peer out the window and find sheep grazing in the pasture. The raven caws, reminding me of his presence. He fans his feathers, but he has nothing to give me. This is the third time this month he's returned without a message. A knot twists in my belly. I know I promised Senga I'd stay away from The Brittle Forest and The Blackhouse, but I fear for her safety more than ever.

My love for Senga precedes any memory I have of her. It's always been there, even before I found out about our betrothal. It's not something I know, but something I *feel*, with every bone in my body, like the sting of nettle or the pinch of too-tight boots.

Every morning is the same as I ready myself for the day. I imagine Senga dashing through the glen, over the hills, and into my arms. Perhaps it's foolish, but I hold onto the candle of hope gleaming inside me, cheering me through the darkest storms.

If not for the raven rousing me awake this morning, I might've missed her. A lonesome creature hanging on the horizon, caught between beast and beauty, her scarlet hair wreathed in mist. As she draws closer, I can't believe my eyes. She's not a figment of my imagination or a dream I love to ravish. She's as real as the blood coursing through my veins.

I dash to the front door and fling it open. "Senga!" I shout. She looks like a ghost risen from the grave, cold as ice and caked in blood. "Were you in The Brittle Forest last night?"

She hangs her head in shame.

"When the raven came back without a message, I nearly broke my promise and came looking for you. I was so worried."

"I'm glad you didn't," she rasps. "It's better you don't know what happens in The Brittle Forest."

"Did your family make a sacrifice to Kilda?"

She takes a wary step towards me, then another. "Whatever sacrifice my family made, I'm just as guilty. I'm not like you, Ivor. I'm not a good person."

"Don't say that. It's not true."

"It *is* true, but I'm worn to the last thread," Senga says hoarsely. "I don't want to cause you any trouble, but I can't go back to The Blackhouse."

She looks at me, soft and broken open. I can't resist her any longer, not when she's this close to me. I twine my arms around her shivering body.

"You don't ever have to go back to The Blackhouse. You can stay with me for as long as you want. You're chilled to the bone. Come and sit by the fire."

Too tired to protest, she follows me inside, dragging her feet behind her. "I promise I won't be a bother for long."

"You're never a bother," I reassure her. I kindle a fire quickly, coaxing the coals with an old trick my father taught me.

Senga sits down by the hearth. "I ran away from Lorna and Gunn last night. They may already be looking for me. I don't want to put you in danger, but I don't have anywhere else to go. You know I'm not welcome anywhere else on this isle." She takes a ragged breath, rubbing her hands together. "After a night's rest, I'll go to the shipyard and sail away."

I kneel beside her, squeezing her hand. "Please, don't ever sail away without me." My voice rises like a prayer.

Senga peels off her soggy cape and lays it beside the hearth. After kicking off her boots and socks, she relaxes into the chair and warms her feet by the fire.

I fill a copper pot with water and hang it over the flames. "Everything you need for a cup of tea is right behind you. Help yourself while I find you something dry to wear."

"Thank you, Ivor."

I set my sights on the armoire in search of comfortable attire. Granted, it's awkward sorting through Mina's garments, but she has no use for them anymore. Besides, nothing of mine would even come close to fitting Senga. After several minutes of rifling, I settle on a gown, a bulky sweater, and long wool socks.

When I return, Senga is half-asleep. The room is all aglow, cinders dancing in the fire. I gently touch her shoulder, offering her a handful of garments. "These should do the trick."

Senga winces at the sight of them. "Will nothing of yours fit me?"

"I'm afraid not."

She crinkles her nose. "Don't get me wrong. I'm grateful, but isn't it rather unseemly of me to wear Mina's garments? The last thing I need is to insult the dearly departed."

I crack a smile. "Desperate times call for desperate measures. Besides, she'll never know. I laid her to rest properly, so her ghost shouldn't be milling about."

Senga muses for a moment. "Well, it would be nice to wear something clean and warm after walking through the mud and rain all night. I must look awfully haggard."

"You look beautiful," I say reassuringly, my dead eye flickering.

Senga bites back a laugh, pulling a rumpled leaf from her hair. "Beautiful or not, I need a good scrub."

“Here, let me help you,” I offer, filling a bowl with warm water. Senga shuts her eyes and surrenders to the heat of the crackling fire. I wet the sponge and press it to her brow, making little circles around her cheeks, dipping down her neck, washing away the grime.

Senga leans forward, responding to my touch. She drops her shoulders and rests her neck between my knees. She’s so close to the edge of my desire, to the length I want to slip inside her, that I can hardly breathe. A howl stirs in my throat, waking the wulver inside me. I grit my teeth, tamping down my urges.

I grab a brush from the table and wet it with warm water. “I’ll be as gentle as I can with the tangles,” I say, running the brush through her hair. When I come across a clump of mud, she murmurs under her breath, trying not to flinch as I loosen it.

When her hair is smooth and clean, she looks up and smiles at me. “Close your eyes so I can change.”

Behind closed eyes, sparks fly through me. How badly I want her, to peel back her petals and taste her sweet nectar, to grab her hip bones and thrust myself inside her. I want to feel her quake with pleasure.

“You can open your eyes now,” Senga breathes, her lips toying with my ear. When I open my eyes, she’s wearing the gown and nothing more. She inches closer, so close I can see the freckles on her cheeks. "I've wanted to be alone with you for so long."

"Me too," I whisper, lowering my gaze to the swell of her breasts and her nipples, red as roses.

Senga leans into me, bruising my neck with a kiss. Rain pelts the roof, hard and wet, as she hikes the gown up over her hips. She arches her back as I caress the dip of her spine. I wait a beat, following her lead, blood rushing through me.

She squeezes my hand and presses it against the cushion of her thigh, invitingly soft and warm. I creep through her secret garden, my fingers finding her slippery blossom. She shudders as I touch her there, again and again, stirring her into a frenzy. Her breath urges me on, needful and uneven, her thighs trembling with the first hint of release. The sound she makes is enough to undo me, the wet whispers of a fallen angel. I watch as she reels with shocks of pleasure, digging her nails into my shoulders, dragging her teeth along my ear.

Rougher now, she tumbles into me. She grabs my jaw and kisses me, her teeth sharp as thorns. I lick a drop of blood from my lips, my heart racing rabbit-quick. I clutch her hips, spinning her onto my lap. What a sweet torment as she rocks against me, her nipples grazing my lips. She tilts her head back, baring her neck for me. A hiss escapes her lips as I sink my teeth into her pale flesh.

Smooth as honey, she slips her hand under my belt, gripping my length. My throat rolls with thunder; my body floods with heat. The room spins to black, blurring my vision. I feel the strangest sensations: skin and bones shifting, muscles surging, fur prickling down my spine, fangs piercing my gums.

The moment is almost perfect, but *almost* isn't enough. I twist away from her, a violent ache pulsing through me.

"Don't you want to?" Senga asks, her voice shadowy with worry.

"More than anything," I say reassuringly, catching my breath. "But you're vulnerable, with no one else to turn to. I don't want you to think that you owe me something just because I let you stay here. If we're going to be together, I want you to feel at home first."

"I think that's the sweetest thing anyone has ever said to me," Senga smiles, her eyes green as tea leaves. "Just promise not to make me wait too long."

I lace her fingers through mine. "Only if you promise to never sail away without me."

"I promise," she whispers.

# 39

## Senga

What a difference happiness makes; time seems to fly on silver wings. For eight moons, I've made myself at home with Ivor. Much to my surprise, Lorna and Gunn haven't come looking for me. Perhaps they're glad I'm gone. Despite the security Ivor gives me, I still have moments when I feel like a rabbit caught in a trap. I've stolen two of Kilda's sacrifices, and I fear her wrath.

Ivor walks beside me under the gloaming. Waves lap against our boots as we squish through the sand. I draw a floral breath, the air sweet with summer roses. I tell myself the worst is over, that everything before I came to Ivor's croft was just a bad dream. I tell myself to put it all behind me: my mother and father, Diarmid and Abilene.

A sound catches on the wind. With each heartbeat, it grows louder. I wonder if Ivor hears it too: the cry of singing wounds.

Not a day goes by that I don't think of Abilene. I consider how many times she could've killed me when we were all alone in The Tide Pools. She could've drowned me, held me underwater until I stopped kicking. She could've cracked my head open on the rocks. She could've snapped my neck with her bare hands. She could've bled me dry with her savage fangs. But she never did any of those things; she tried to help me, instead.

I still dream of the waterspout spinning around me. I feel the poke of the needle and the pull of the thread as I stitch my legs together. Some nights, I even feel my phantom tail tangled up in the sheets.

Ivor creeps up behind me, burying his nose in the upsweep of my hair. He lingers there, bringing me back to the present. I whirl around, and he holds me with hungry eyes. We've been awake since dawn fishing and digging for clams. I rub my aching back, welcoming the pain. There's something sorely delicious about a hard day's work with Ivor – all the salt and sun, wind and rain, sweating and panting. And best of all, it does my heart good to know we have food for the landies.

When we reach our secret spot near the sea caves, we wedge our nets and pails between the rocks. Ivor kindles a fire while I spread a blanket over the sand. My pulse quickens as I lean back and undress, anticipating what's to come. I long to be in Ivor's arms, naked as the moon in the sky. I want him to crash into me like waves on the shore, but I haven't let him inside me yet.

As much as I give, I hold back, secrets buried in my heart deeper than roots. Secrets that would tear us apart if he knew the truth. I stare out into the misty sea, wishing it wasn't true, but I know I'm wicked through and through.

I've captured mermaids and watched my family torture and kill them. I let my father drown and my mother sacrifice herself in The Brittle Forest. I watched Diarmid die and helped burn his body like an animal on an altar. I withheld the truth from his grieving widow. I dreamt of poisoning Mina when she was alive, and I was happy when she died.

My teeth ache, and I realize I'm clenching my jaw. I open wide, releasing the tension, banishing the shadows from my heart. Ivor edges towards me, his eyes glowing in the dark. He kicks off his socks and boots and unfastens his belt. His tunic sails through the air, landing between my thighs. The scent of him drifts on the breeze: crisp pine and spiced wood. I reach out, pulling him on top of me.

He slants his mouth over the crescent of my collarbone, leaving me with a feeling like no other. A flame between my thighs, climbing higher and higher. After a whispery bite, he glides his lips down my navel and further, teasing the ribbons of flesh between my thighs. I bury my hands in his hair, black as midnight. He peels me apart, petal by petal, until he reaches the center. Slow at first, then fast and fierce, he licks me into a frenzy.

"Ivor," I gasp, coming undone. I wrap my legs around him, spiraling towards a blessed release. He lingers between my thighs while waves of pleasure wash over me. Then he climbs me like a vine, tilts my jaw, and kisses me.

I kiss him back, dragging my lips down his neck and further until my mouth is below his navel. He crushes my hair between his fingers, begging me to return the favor. I gaze up at him, my mouth full, my eyes glittering hot. I glide back and forth, keeping a steady rhythm.

He pants in the rough of his throat, a sound more animal than human, like a beast tearing meat from the bone. On the brink of pleasure, he clutches my collarbone and howls.

In the afterglow, I rest my head on his chest, his heart pounding in my ear. My sweat quickly turns to chill. Ivor warms me up, smoothing his hands down my spine. It feels good until his thumb grazes my scars; I flinch away from him. I can't see his face, but I can feel his questions. He wants to know everything about me, even my scars.

I'm jumpy now, thinking about my father and the harp strings. A ghost crab skitters across my foot. It reminds me of my mother, a touch so faint I can't even be sure it's there. When I close my eyes, I see her running through a meadow, a crown of fairy bells in her hair. The lilt of her voice haunts me, rasping in my ear.

*I loved a mermaid once.*

Who did my mother love all those years ago? What happened to her heavenly voice? Did someone steal it from her? Was it my father? Kilda? Lorna? All these questions and more burn inside me, but I'll never know the answers.

# 40

## Earie

The old eel swells inside me, his jagged teeth tickling me pink. I toss my head back, mid-gasp, scraping my coral antlers on the reef. The old eel knows all my memories; he sifts through them, poking them at the seams. It feels good until he rakes his tail over the most painful one. I beg him to stop, but he won't, not until his pleasure is spent.

I rub the hag stone around my neck, an old, sad song filling my ears as the past comes rushing back to me.

I'm lying on The Crooked Sands, sheets of rain pouring from the sky. A voice cries out, muffled by the wind. I can't be sure, but it sounds human. Could it be Twila after all this time? I hold my breath, bracing for disappointment. It's been thirty-seven moons since I've seen her.

The voice calls out again, my name ringing clear as a bell. I dig my palms into the sand, raising myself up as high as I can. A sail pierces the gloom on the edge of The Cauldron. Squinting through the rain, I catch a glimpse of a hooded figure. A gust of wind blows through her cape, revealing a web of mahogany hair, and my breath hitches at the sight.

"Twila!" I shout, my heart in my throat. I scramble through the shallows, cutting myself on the shell-washed sand. I swim past the breakers as fast as I can. I crest each wave as it comes, fixing my eyes on the lugger.

Twila leans over the bow and drops the anchor. A heartbeat later, she jumps into the sea. Deep waters roll around us. I catch hold of her waist and fin for The Crooked Sands, taking great pains to keep her head above the water.

When we reach the black sand, Twila lets out a violent cough. “I’ve missed you so much,” she whispers, shivering in my arms.

“I’ve missed you too. I was afraid something terrible happened to you. I swam to Wulver Cove and searched for you, even though Gran Opal warned me not to.”

Twila brushes her hand through my hair, snagging her thumb on a coral antler. She presses her wound to my mouth and I lick away the blood. After all this time, she still tastes divine. Twila lets out a ragged breath, her eyes widening. “Tonight is the first chance I’ve had to escape the castle. Lorna isn’t my sister anymore; she’s a monster. She gave herself to a bluebeard, and they’ve shackled my father in the dungeon. Worst of all, Lorna threatened to kill my father if I didn’t marry a bluebeard.” Twila grabs my wrists, her nails biting my flesh. “I’m sorry, Earie. I never wanted to marry Warr. He’s a wicked man. I should’ve fought harder against it, but I was afraid of what they would do to my father.”

I press my forehead against hers. “It’s not your fault, Twila. You’re not to blame for what happened. I can put an end to your pain. I can take you to The Deep Dark Nether. You can wait with my sisters until I can join you." My voice surges, all waves and power. I lift her chin, surprising her with a kiss. "I'm stronger than I was before. I know I can inherit The Deep Dark Nether. We can have what we've always wanted. We can be together forever." I clutch her hips and pull her closer.

Twila flashes a bruised smile. "I'm glad you believe in yourself the way I do, truly, I am, but it's too late for me, Earie. I can't leave my daughter."

"*Your daughter?*" I choke on the words, my tentacles coiling around her.

"Senga, my little thistle," she whispers, her amber eyes glistening with tears. "I only came to say goodbye to you."

"This can't be the end. There must be another way. I'd rather die than live without you." My vision darkens as I search for a solution. "What if I swim to Wulver Cove and wait for you there while you get Senga and your father? I can take you all to The Deep Dark Nether and we can be a family together," I coax, desperate to persuade her.

Twila lowers her gaze. "It's too dangerous. My father is shackled in the dungeon, and there's no way for me to release him. And if Warr caught me trying to escape with Senga, he might kill her or my father just to punish me." She leans into me, tracing her fingers down my spine and around my tail. "Besides, I shudder to think of what Kilda would do if you tried to help me. Your sisters need you, and I need you, too. You're our only hope, Earie."

Dread settles in my tentacles. In the space of a breath, I bury myself in her arms, inhaling the fragrance of her hair. "If I had taken you to The Deep Dark Nether when you asked me to, none of this would've ever happened."

Twila pales, wringing her hands. "Lorna and the bluebeards will wake soon. I should return to the castle before sunrise, but I want to give you something first."

Tears burn in my eyes. "You don't have to give me anything. All I've ever wanted is your love."

"You have my love, now and forever, but I want to give you something more, a piece of me so we can always be together." She pauses, her lips grazing the shell of my ear. "When did you know you loved me?"

"From the moment I heard your voice."

Twila smiles sweetly, her long lashes fluttering. "If I ask you to do something for me, will you do it without hesitation?"

"Yes. Anything."

Twila lies down in the sand and closes her eyes, snuffing out the only light I've ever known. "Then these will be the last words between us – take my voice and wear it close to your heart forever."

I gasp, her words lingering like an endless night. "Are you sure?"

She nods, tears glittering down her cheeks.

I swallow hard, my hands pale knives against her face. "Sing for me," I whisper.

Twila parts her lips and haunts me with her song. All guts and hiss, I bare my fangs in a violent kiss, biting away her pain. I tear her voice from her throat, petal by petal, dark and sweet as a bloody rose. Her song throbs in my mouth, the force nearly breaking my jaw.

When I pull away, Twila gazes up at me, her angel eyes beaming. I slip the hag stone into my mouth and a shiver swims through me as it absorbs her voice.

Dawn breaks like a mirror, pale light scattering around us. I nudge Twila and we splash through the shallows, dodging a swarm of jellyfish. As we swim deeper, rough waves batter us. Twila gasps for breath, clinging to me as I fin for the lugger.

The world is a wet blur, my heart aching with nevermore. The memory sails away, taking my true love with it. I throw myself on a moss-slick rock and cry. Love is nothing more than a long goodbye.

# 41

## Ivor

Senga lies in my arms, the moon shining bright as a pearl. We just returned from a long night of deliveries. Our muscles ache, but the pain is worth it. The landies will be so happy when they wake up and find baskets on their doorsteps, overflowing with lobsters, clams, and hake.

Our first stop was the northern shore, home to Lady Mirren, the old spinstress. We visited many homes along the eastern shore before reaching The Teahouse. We left baskets for Sir Craig, Lady Graham, and bareback Bonnie. And we left little Aila a handful of shrimp, of course, for it's her favourite.

As we neared the last stop, Senga halted, her smile fading. She hid in the shadows with Broon while I left a basket on Sorcha's doorstep. I almost asked her what was wrong, but I knew it would only upset her.

The question is still on my mind; I wish Senga would tell me what she's hiding. If ever there was a time to spill secrets, it would be now, curled up in the black sand, the curve of her hip in my hand.

Senga moves ever so slightly, tempting me with ribs and nipples. She rests her lips on my neck, with a touch so light it's barely perceptible, and yet the effect is maddening. A surge of need rushes through me. My thoughts drift to last night, and the night before, and all things we do in the dark. Senga's red hair flaming against ivory peaks and mossy valleys. Her jaw stretched wide, absorbing my length. The bend of her neck smoothing over me. The sound she makes when I lick her into a frenzy.

A sheep bleats near The Tide Pools. I snap to attention, welcoming the distraction.

Senga sits up and lifts the lantern. "Is that a sheep?"

"I think so," I say, raising up beside her. "There's a strange flock that comes here every summer. They've taken a liking to the kelp."

She smiles, but it's a thin disguise. Her secrets are eating her from the inside out. I can see it in her eyes; they creep towards the sea, sick and green with guilt. "Can I take your skiff out tomorrow? There's somewhere I need to go."

I raise a brow. "Where?"

Senga crinkles her nose in a pained expression.

"I could go with you," I offer.

She squirms, biting her lip. "It's too dangerous. I'd never forgive myself if something happened to you."

"If it's *that* dangerous, then I insist on coming with you. We can take the lugger. It has more room, and it'll be safer."

"Yes, but the skiff is easier to hide."

"It seems you're hiding a lot of things," I whisper.

Senga sighs, wringing her hands. "I want to tell you *everything*, Ivor, really, I do, but I'm afraid of losing you."

I lift her chin, swimming in her emerald eyes. "I've loved you from the cradle, and I'll love you to the grave. You can tell me anything, Senga. Nothing will ever change the way I feel about you."

She falls into my arms, softer than ever before: all petals, no thorns. "There's so much to tell. I don't even know where to start."

"You could start with what happened to Diarmid. I saw how troubled you were at Sorcha's house tonight."

With a shaky breath, Senga reaches for my hand, something giving way inside her. "I saw Diarmid the day he died. He came to The Blackhouse shortly after I lost my mother and father." She pauses, mustering the courage to continue. "Diarmid confronted Lorna. He told her that he suspected Gunn was responsible for the cloven bodies and for what happened to my mother and father. Diarmid was hellbent on sailing to the mainland to expose Gunn's wicked deeds. Lorna was desperate to stop him, but she couldn't, so she laced his tea with wolfsbane."

A vein throbs in my neck. "*Lorna* killed Diarmid?"

"Yes, she's every bit as wicked as Gunn. I swear I didn't know what she was doing. I tried to help Diarmid, but it was too late. After he died, Lorna threatened your life if I told anyone what happened," Senga cries, the fragile edge of her voice breaking.

"Oh, Senga," I whisper, grabbing her tight, digging my fingers deep. She winces and I loosen my grip, a bruise blooming between her ribs.

She rubs the tender spot, secrets still pouring from her lips. "The cloven women weren't women at all, but mermaids. My family hunts them every summer during The Mooring, but you knew that already, didn't you?" she asks softly.

"I had my suspicions. I tried to stop the bluebeards many times, but I never succeeded. I wanted to protect you more than anything, but I let you down. I'm so sorry."

"You don't have anything to be sorry for, Ivor. You've been nothing but kind to me and everyone on this isle," she soothes, rubbing my shoulder. "You're the only friend I've ever had, apart from Abilene."

"Who's Abilene?" I ask.

"She's the mermaid we captured last summer. When my mother was sick, I took Abilene to The Tide Pools every week. She told me a story about a brave wulver who tried to help the mermaids." Senga squeezes my hand, her words lingering in the air. "It was *you*, wasn't it? You're the wulver from Abilene's story?"

I nod, meeting her gaze.

"And it was my father who mangled your eye and slayed your family, wasn't it?"

I nod again and she shivers. "I don't hold you responsible for what your father did. You're nothing like him," I reassure her.

"I tried to set Abilene free, but my father caught us before she could escape. They fought to the bitter end, tearing each other to ribbons." Senga goes pale, her hair whipping in the wind. "And without Abilene, we didn't have a sacrifice for Kilda. Gunn was furious with me. He thought I should go to The Brittle Forest and sacrifice myself to Kilda, but my mother insisted on taking my place." Senga chokes the words out, her eyes brimming with tears.

I press my forehead to hers, threading my fingers through her hair. "My father put himself in harm's way to protect me, too. I used to think it was my fault that he died, but I realize now that it wasn't. I was up against monsters that I couldn't slay, no matter how hard I tried. But I didn't let that stop me from doing what I could and neither did you. You're the reason Abilene made it back to the sea; you're the one who set her free. Freedom always comes at a cost."

Senga nods, wiping the tears from her eyes. "Abilene showed me my true nature. I saw it when I looked in her mirror. I had silver scales and my neck was laced with gills." She looks up at me, gauging my reaction. "Do you believe in our true nature?"

"With all my heart," I whisper, a howl stirring in my throat.

A smile skims her lips. Just when I think she's going to kiss me, she looks down, wearing her lashes like a veil. "I must go to The Mooring tomorrow. I can't let Lorna and Gunn capture another mermaid. I know where they like to hunt on Crescent Isle. If I can get there before they do and hide the skiff, then I might be able to stop them."

"You mean *we* might be able to stop them. I'm going with you," I insist, flashing a wolfish smile.

"It'll be dangerous, Ivor. We might not survive."

I cradle her in my arms, kissing the pulse of her throat. "I'd rather die with you, fighting for our ancestors, than live without you."

# 42

## Abilene

It's a strange thing, to be a soul without a shell. My spirit floats in The Deep Dark Nether, sensing the scattered bits and pieces of my body. Here's the sharp line of my shoulder blade, the shark-toothed scars even prettier than I remember. Overhead, my skin hangs from a line of kelp, pearl-white and glistening. On the highest shelf, my voice hisses in a glass jar. Buried beneath the rocks, my heart pounds, and my tongue sings. Deep in the shadows, my rosy hair sways with the eelgrass. Around the corner, my bones have become one with the tallest pile.

I'm not alone; there are others here with me. Sometimes, we bump into each other, all whispering lips and floating ears. Together, we brave the darkest stretch of night, waiting for Earie to sing our bones eternal.

But The Mooring is upon us, and Earie is in trouble. Somewhere in these holy waters, my fingers are conjuring dark little magic. I know not where, but I can feel it. My soul stirs, a force to be reckoned with, as I cast my dreams on Senga. I'll never forget what she did for me and Thora, and we need her – now, more than ever.

# 43

## The Mermaid Chorus

It starts with a scream – a dire plea from a desperate creature. She thrashes in The Bitter Sea, wild-eyed and skinny.

"I'm almost there, just a little lower!" Gunn shouts, lifting his head towards the lugger. The sun peeks through the clouds, painting the sky warm gold.

Lorna blows a wisp of hair from her eyes, keeping her hands firmly planted on the ghost rope.

"I've got her!" Gunn catches the desperate creature by her elbow. She fangs his arm, but he isn't afraid of her. He grabs her by the throat, her face turning an ugly blue, starving for air. His frown deepens as he looks her over. Her chest is flat as a board, her eyes young and green. "She's just a merchild, Lorna! She can't be the queenfish!"

"She'll have to do for now. Keep hold of her, and I'll pull you up!" Lorna yells, tugging on the ghost rope – until it slips from her hands. With a great splash, Gunn smacks the skin of the sea.

A voice calls from the deep. Gunn whirls around, tracing the source.

"*I'm the queenfish*, you mangy beast," Earie hisses, cresting a giant wave. She stares him down, fangs bared, skin hanging from her bones. She wears a crown of deadly creatures and a veil of black tentacles. They grin at Gunn with glass-sharp teeth.

Gunn falters, losing his grip on the merchild, and she wrenches herself free. She swims over to Earie, beating her tail against the waves. "My mother was willing to die for you, and so am I."

"I won't hear of it, Thora," Earie answers. "The bluebeards have already taken enough from our family. Swim back to your father, and he'll mend your wound."

Thora crosses her arms, looking defiant.

"I'm your queenfish; do as I tell you," Earie bids.

Thora bows her head and plunges deep beneath the waves.

At once, clouds swell, turning the sky a darker grey. Gunn flings the ghost rope at Earie, catching her by the neck. She tries to tear it away, but to no avail. With a nasty snort, Gunn kicks her with his hooves, knocking the wind out of her. But her tentacles are quick to punish him: they sting him beyond measure.

With a watchful eye, Lorna creeps to the edge of the lugger. She sucks a daring breath, posing for a dive.

"Don't do it, Lorna," Gunn warns, flailing in the water.

Lorna pays him no mind and jumps into the sea.

"You should've stayed in the lugger, Lorna. You can't help me," Gunn chokes, his breath shaky and uneven.

"I didn't drench myself on your behalf, you fool," Lorna snaps, rubbing the salt from her eyes.

"You're as good as dead, and I'm glad to be rid of you." She lifts her chin above the water with a triumphant smile. "Now I don't have to share any of the glory with you."

Gunn's expression twists, as though he's just tasted something sour. He reaches for Lorna's hand, but she yanks it away. Her lips curl in disgust at the sight of his face: a mess of popping flesh, worsening by the second.

"Lorna," he rasps, but his cry falls on deaf ears.

With startling strength, Lorna sculls away, leaving him to drown, setting her sights on the queenfish. "What do we have here?" she sneers, her eyes upon Earie. "Are *you* the queenfish? How can it be?" Lorna tosses her head with a tart laugh. "You're the ugliest thing I've ever seen."

Earie bristles, unleashing her tentacles.

Lorna rolls her eyes and swats them away. "I'm not afraid of you, devilfish. I have the same gift my sister had – *immunity*. Twila used her gift to love you, and I'm going to use mine to kill you."

*Immunity*. The word dawns on Earie, brighter than the sun. She trembles, her spine rising like a sail.

Lorna twines her arms around Earie's waist. "How long has it been since you've been in the pink? Without my sister, you must be *terribly lonely*. I can touch you just the way she did. I can leave you spiraling with pleasure," Lorna taunts, grabbing Earie's jaw and giving her a brutal kiss.

Earie twists away, reaching for the nest of stinging creatures in her hair, but the stonefish is asleep, just like her tentacles. She tries to hold Lorna's head underwater, but her hands are too weak.

"Is that all you've got?" Lorna dissolves into a mocking laugh. She grabs a tentacle and squeezes it. "Positively delicious," she swoons, licking the venom from her fingers. One by one, she grabs and drains each tentacle.

Defenseless, Earie lets out a weak hiss, panic setting in. With a violent shiver, her vision blurs. Her world is darker than ever before, sable stars and eternal night all around her, but she refuses to surrender. She stirs and fights back, sinking her fangs into Lorna's arm.

Lorna tears away, pulling a blade from her boot. She raises it high above her head. For a beat, it hangs in the air, pale-silver, then she plunges it into Earie's chest.

The sea rolls red with death.

Earie clenches her jaw, biting back the pain. Despite her agony, she refuses to give Lorna the pleasure of a scream.

*This is the end.*

Earie feels it, a chill settling in her bones, her verve slipping away. She squeezes the hag stone around her neck, her fingers slick with blood. She drifts for a moment, dreaming of Twila, when a sharp pain rouses her awake. She feels the ghost rope burning her tail as Lorna drags her through the water.

Earie clings to a single word: *escape*. She must escape before Lorna tosses her into the lugger and sacrifices her to Kilda. She squirms and writhes, twisting to break free.

Lorna yanks on the ghost rope even harder, desperate to capture the queenfish. Preoccupied with the struggle, she doesn't notice the skiff sneaking up on them, nor does she notice the wulver slipping beneath the waves – until he snatches the ghost rope from her hands.

Lorna spins around and her nose is all but pressed against Ivor's. He stares at her grimly, his dead eye flickering. She clutches Earie's tail, but Ivor rips her hands away, her bones cracking. She screams in pain as Ivor steals the queenfish from her.

Senga pulls Earie into the lugger and Ivor follows. He drops to his knees and presses his hands against Earie's bleeding heart.

Senga looks down, glaring at Lorna. "What have you done?"

"I captured the queenfish." Lorna kicks her tired legs to stay afloat, still managing to sneer. "I'm taking her to The Brittle Forest, and you and Ivor are sailing back to Wulver Cove."

"Like hell we are," Ivor snarls.

Lorna ignores him, fixing her cruel eyes on Senga. "I know you, Senga Thistle. You'll do as I say, as you've always done. Now give me the queenfish or I'll tell Ivor what *you* did to Diarmid."

"*I* didn't do anything to Diarmid! *You* did!" Senga jumps into the sea, grabbing a fistful of blonde hair and slamming Lorna against the skiff.

Lorna reels from the blow, gritting her teeth, spitting blood into the water. "You're as guilty as I am, Senga. My blood runs through your veins."

"Then it's high time I wash you out of me," Senga says with an icy smile. "I'm here to do what my mother should've done a long time ago."

Lorna tries to wrench away, but Senga grabs her even tighter. Earie lets out a desperate cry, mustering every ounce of her strength. She plucks a black urchin from a hidey hole in her hair and hands it to Senga.

Senga grips the urchin in her hand like a knife, blood dripping from her fingers. She stares at Lorna, her cold eyes gleaming.

Lorna shudders, paling with fright. Before she can draw another breath, she sees red, *feels red*. Pain explodes inside her, a hundred needles stabbing her neck, as the urchin's spines gore her flesh. Utterly exhausted, her legs give out on her.

How different humans look when they realize they're not invincible, how sad and small and frightened.

As Lorna sinks, the fog rolls in, thick as smoke. The last of her floats on the skin of the sea, her honey-blonde hair the only proof she ever existed.

Earie flops to the edge of the skiff, waving a hand at Ivor. He scoops her up in his arms and jumps into the water.

Earie bobs next to Senga, flashing a blood-smeared smile. “I know who you are, Senga. You’re a black pearl from The Bitter Sea, just like your mother.”

“You knew my mother?”

“She was my true love,” Earie says sadly. “She gave me her voice so we could always be together. Listen.” Earie presses the hag stone to Senga’s ear.

Senga closes her eyes, her mind creeping through the shadows, where lost things lurk around every corner: her mother singing a faraway song. The smell of fairy bells and dark little magic. The beauty of harps and strings, the way they were meant to be before they cut her to the bone.

Senga trembles as she rubs her fingers over the hag stone. When her eyes flutter open, she meets Earie’s violet gaze. “My mother is trapped in The Brittle Forest, and it’s all my fault. She sacrificed herself for me.”

“That’s what mothers do – they die so their daughters might live.” Earie strains, the words catching in her throat. “I’m fading fast, but there’s a place for you in The Deep Dark Nether. Throw yourself below the salt and call on me.” Earie wheezes, her eyes rolling back in her skull, then she slips beneath the waves.

Senga buries her face in Ivor’s chest, their tears mingling.

Fast blows the wind, carrying the news to Kilda. With Earie on the brink of death, ready to claim The Deep Dark Nether, Kilda knows all hope is lost. There's nothing left to do but weep, and weep she does, as her trunk turns to dust.

# 44

## Senga

Under the starry sky, our bodies break against the waves. A cloud turns over, drenching us with rain. Our wounds touch at last, dark little magic spilling from our veins.

Ivor feels the shift before I do. He snaps his head back, his jaw striking a harsh angle. Fur sprouts on his chest and spreads down his spine. What big eyes and fierce fangs, hungry enough to eat me. I crest a wave, rolling with his body. I feel the heat of muscles and bones shifting. He responds in turn, nibbling my neck. Something tingles beneath his tongue, a thing of wonder.

*Gills*.

What a curious sensation, air and water flowing through me. I slip my fingers between the folds, lace-thin and ticklish. I glide my hands over the meat of my tail as the needle and thread stitch my legs together.

Ivor clutches my waist. Lifts me to his mouth. Finds the aching slit between my scales. He teases me with playful nips as a hot breath escapes my lips. I wait for him to undo me, but he holds back, fixing me with his feral eyes.

"I love you," he says, his voice a weathered rock I want to cling to.

"I love you, too," I whisper.

We embrace each other, bobbing in the sea. Gore drips from my fingers and down his shoulders. Even the water can't wash away the berry-red blood of Lorna and Earie.

Ivor searches me, his dead eye flickering. “Are you ready to call on the queenfish?”

Awareness simmers inside me, dread bubbling to the surface. “You can’t go with me, can you?”

His expression darkens. A waterspout looms on the horizon, the same one from my dreams.

“I don’t want to go without you,” I hiss, wrapping my tail around him, a prisoner of my own memories. I think of the summer solstice. The scent of smoke and roses. The thrill of our first kiss in the sea caves when he pulled me underwater. Stormy nights together, tangled in the sheets, the candles burning low. I close my eyes, clinging to him as though he might disappear forever.

Ivor presses his forehead to mine, roughing me with his whiskers. “I don’t want you to go either, but this isn’t goodbye,” he soothes. “My father told me that all creatures live as one under the full moon.”

I breathe a sigh of relief, though I’m not quite sure what he means.

“When the moon is full, I’ll meet you in the sea caves,” Ivor vows, threading his fingers through my hair. “Promise you’ll meet me there.”

“I promise,” I say.

He smiles, his eyes crinkling at the corners. He longs for consummation, but he restrains himself, true to his noble nature.

I let out a ragged breath before I slip under. As I glide through the inky water, an impulse tempts me. I spin around and swim back to Ivor, stealing a glimpse of his submerged anatomy. Much to my delight, he still has the length of a man to please me.

I rise, breaking the skin of the sea. Ivor turns and finds me soft for digging. “A month is a long time to wait,” I whisper, flicking my tongue at him.

“An eternity,” he smiles, eyeing my lips.

Everything comes so naturally in the water; the waves send us crashing into each other. I grab the scruff of his neck, crushing his fur between my fingers. I reach for the clouds. Twist his jaw to my mouth. Press him hard with a kiss, a kiss so fierce it bruises his lips.

I spread my arms like wings, floating effortlessly on the water. Ivor watches for a beat as I roll the waves. Eager to please me, he drags a claw over my breastbone, tracing the shape of my heart. Then he roughs me with his tongue, licking beads of salt from my nipples.

With a sultry smile, I slide out from under him. I sweep my palm below his navel and take him in my hand. Tightening my grip, I apply just enough pressure, maddening him beyond measure.

Fangs bared, he snags my ear, muttering curses and blessings, aching with a terrible need for more. He clutches my waist. Finds my lonely slit and buries his length inside me. I curl my spine with a wild hiss, making room for him. It only hurts for a breath. Now I'm soft and broken open, gliding with him in perfect rhythm.

He wears me skin-tight, his claws whittling my waist. I shower him with wet whispers, spiraling into a blessed release. His pleasure isn't far behind. He slants his mouth over mine, panting against me. He howls and I hiss, the smell of earth and pine on his skin.

For a moment in time, our world is a beautiful blur of kisses and promises. The sea cradles us in its wrinkles, rocks us in its wisdom.

I belong here, but Ivor doesn't.

The bitter truth steals my breath away. The storm rages even harder, all bleak sky and endless rain. I urge Ivor into the skiff, my heart pounding with the waves.

Then I blink and he's gone, the winds of change ever blowing. Gulls fly high above me, singing an old, sad song. Lightning strikes, brightening the gloom, and that's when I see it.

*The waterspout spinning around me.*

# 45

## Senga

The dream is here, but I'm awake. In the eye of the storm, there's no escape. On the edge of the waterspout, I know these things to be true: I'm a black pearl from The Bitter Sea, and only courage can set me free. I plunge beneath the waves, dropping my tail like an anchor. Abilene's song echoes in my memory; my lips move, reciting the words she taught me.

*Sing we angelfish on high.*
*Sing we of The Deep Dark Nether.*
*Sing our tongues of blood.*
*Sing our bones eternal.*

Suddenly, an inky swirl catches my eye, and I feel tentacles squeezing me, dragging me deeper through rings of blue. Swarms of jellyfish drift through the watery sky while my life flashes before my eyes.

This is how it feels to die – the moment I realize I'm no longer a bright bud but a crushed flower, the seams of my soul threadbare. I'm falling away, the sea a silent altar, and I'm the prayer.

When my eyes flutter open, I see a graveyard. Piles of skulls and spines and heartless rib cages. Candles gleaming and glass jars humming with voices. But the prettiest sight of all is a bony hand reaching out from behind a seaweed curtain.

*The queenfish.*

Earie floats on a throne of cockleshells, combing her pitch-black hair. With a bubbly breath, she meets my gaze, all violet eyes and candle bones. She swims over to me, her tentacles trailing behind her. With an upturned palm, she presses her hand to my heart and a streak of moonlight washes me clean. My bloodstains are gone; my wounds are healed. I twirl around in circles, feeling lighter than air.

I feel eyes on me. I hear voices too, but I can't trace their sources. Earie sweeps her hand across my shoulder, sending a warm chill down my spine. She opens her crooked mouth and holds the first note, a hush washing over the sea.

All through the night, Earie sings our bones eternal. Souls rise to greet their bodies, skin and bones dancing all around me. Suddenly, a familiar voice charms my ear; my heart thumps as I squint in the dark. All I can see is a tail, but I recognize its golden glint.

Abilene comes to me in bits and pieces. Her voice bursts from its glass jar. Her rosy hair slithers through the eelgrass. Her heart glides from beneath a rock. Her bones leap from the tallest pile. Once she's stitched back together, she hugs me, threading her fingers through my hair.

"Listen," Abilene whispers.

I shut my eyes, feeling the world beyond my skin. Somewhere in these holy waters, I hear an angel singing, harps without scars, and copper bells ringing.

“Mother,” I cry, tears spilling from my eyes. She passes through me, ghost-like, all shivers and soft light.

Earie inches closer to me and presses the hag stone to my lips. I crack my jaw open, drinking in my mother’s song, hissing with frenzy. She tastes divine, like sugar and cinnamon, lighting me up from the inside.

As I float in The Deep Dark Nether, I sing like never before, my voice melding with my mother’s. Together, we join the chorus of eternals. We sing of blood and sand, of suffering and salvation. We sing of gods and humans and the dark little magic we do to each other.

Heat dances between my ribs and down my spine, toasting me tender. I’m not alone anymore, among the hawthorns and fairies. I’m inside a candlelit shrine, holding hands with my sisters, warming each other with our own little fires.

I’m where I’ve always wanted to be – home, at last. I’m free.

## Acknowledgements

Publishing *Sing Our Bones Eternal* is a dream come true for me. As an underdog from a holler tucked away in Appalachia, my heart is overflowing with gratitude. The thing about underdogs is that they're grateful for each person who helps them along the way. Hence, a long, loving list of acknowledgments.

I'd like to thank R.K. Hart, Charity, Sonja Blanco, and J.C. Greening for walking beside me on my creative journey. Thanks for spotting plot holes, believing in the story inside me, encouraging me to keep going on rough days, and supporting my vision as I crafted this novel.

My beta readers because your feedback was essential and made this book even better than I could've imagined.

A special thanks to Bek, my amazing editor. I can't thank you enough for honoring my voice and my style while helping me grow along the way. You're a salt of the earth person, and I'm grateful to know you.

My husband for exceeding my wildest dreams and loving me so unconditionally.

My dad who works harder than anyone I've ever known and freely gives his family all that he has. My mom for giving me the grit and courage to survive and thrive. My sister and all my friends and family for being a port in the storm that I can always sail home to.

My ancestors, both the quick and the dead, especially my aunt Debbie.

J.C. Greening (cartographer extraordinaire), Chloe Coblentz ("Haunted Chloe") for the hardcover, and Tea Jagodić for the paperback cover. You're all wonderful artists bursting with creativity, and I'm so grateful to feature your art in my debut.

All the incredibly talented authors who've been willing to write a blurb for *Sing Our Bones Eternal* and for making me feel like part of the community. People like you make the world a better place, and I'm honored to know each one of you. Special shout outs to Heather Herrman, Gillian French, Hester Fox, Paulette Kennedy, A.C. Wise, Jennifer Thorne, Ann Fraistat, Alyssa Wees, Cyla Panin, K.L. Cerra, Nicole Willson, Cia Petrichor, Sonja Blanco, R.K. Hart, B.K. Sweeting, Laura Quinn, J.K. Divia, Laura Holt, Julia Lewis, Susan Earlam, and R.M. Brown.

All my SOBE street team members who've encouraged me with their excitement and helped spread the word. I have the best street team out there.

All the readers, reviewers, bloggers, podcasters, and bookstagrammers who've spent time reading, reviewing, getting to know me, and spreading the word. It means so much to me.

For Gris-Gris, my little familiar, who came into my life when I needed her most and has brought me more joy than I ever could've imagined.

## About the Author

Kacey Rayburn lives in the Appalachian Mountains. Born into a family of granny witches and gravediggers, she enjoys long walks in the cemetery. She has a sweet fang for chai tea, mermaids, fairy tales, and folk horror. *Sing Our Bones Eternal* is her debut novel. Her short fiction has appeared in *The Theatre Phantasmagoria*, *Trembling With Fear*, *Myth & Lore Zine*, and *Grim & Gilded.*

Website: www.kaceyrayburn.com
Instagram: @finsandfables
Facebook: KaceyRayburnAuthor
Goodreads: Kacey Rayburn

**A Conversation with Kacey Rayburn and Sonja Blanco, author of *Witch of Ware Woods***

SB: In addition to being a writer, I know you're a voracious reader. What genres are your favourites to read and write?

KR: Magical realism and speculative fiction are some of my favourite genres because they challenge a single view of reality. What one culture considers to be superstitious and supernatural, other cultures consider their everyday normal. I love these genres because they beg the question: what if? What if mermaids are real, for example. These genres encourage us to suspend our judgment and be open to the experiences of different cultures.

I think growing up in Appalachia has also influenced my genre preferences. My granddad and dad were the caretakers of our local cemetery. I grew up believing in ghosts and superstitions and observing families' death rituals, and I wrote eulogies like poetry. It may seem strange to other people, but for my family it was everyday normal.

SB: This is not strange to me at all! I also love peeking behind the veil and have always been fascinated by cemeteries. Are there any other genres that resonate with you?

KR: I'm also an eternal fan of gothic, folk horror, and fairy tales because they're so primal and universal. They tap into our psyches and bring to light a range of human emotions, archetypes, and experiences. I also love these genres because they're powerful conduits for challenging and transforming societal narratives.

SB: *Sing Our Bones Eternal* has a vivid and fantastic world. What was your worldbuilding process for this story?

KR: Many of the places and creatures that appear in *Sing Our Bones Eternal* was inspired by Scottish folklore, such as storm kelpies, bluebeards/blue men of The Minch, wulvers, hag stones, brownies, St. Kilda, The Cauldron, and rowan and hawthorn trees.

Characters and scenes often come to me in my dreams, so I keep a journal by my bed. I was dreaming about the characters and the folklore that appear in *Sing Our Bones Eternal* long before I ever started writing the book.

I had originally envisioned the book taking place in The Greek Islands. I tried writing the story in this setting for several months, but something just wasn't clicking for me. As I grieved the loss of my aunt, who was the heart and soul of our family, I started having vivid dreams, and my dreams took me to Scotland. These dreams inspired me to learn more about my roots and have meaningful conversations with my grandparents.

I'd heard stories as a child, so I knew I had Scottish roots and ancestors, but I wanted to approach my ancestry as an adult with a different understanding than I had as a child. I felt a stirring, something bone-deep inside me, as though my ancestors were calling me home. As the story took shape, I found myself on a journey exploring ancestral hauntings and healing.

One of the most powerful realizations I had was the impact of generational trauma and the ways we hurt and heal each other. I placed my main character, Senga, smack dab in the middle of these realizations. I wanted her to explore complicated emotions. What does it feel like to be torn between loyalty to her family while acknowledging the error in their ways? What does it feel like to do what's right even if she loses someone she loves? What does it feel like to carve her own path and live with all the joy and pain it brings?

SB: What an incredible journey! I love hearing when dreams and family roots influence a writer. It was kismet you felt in your bones, and the magic comes through in your writing. OK, so tell me about your fascination with mermaids.

KR: Mermaids are powerful archetypes. Across space and time, they've captured our hearts. We've feared them and loved them. I've always thought of mermaids as messengers of the deep and symbols of wisdom. I think they teach us to look in the mirror and discover the ghost ropes that bind us, and the ghost ropes we use to bind each other.

An important theme in *Sing Our Bones Eternal* is honoring the common thread that unites us as humans. Though each clan has its own memories, traumas, and strengths, there is one spirit that unites us all.

I also think mermaids are often seen as seductresses, who use their voices to bewitch humans and drown them. In *Sing Our Bones Eternal*, when humans jump into the sea, it's not because the mermaid has bewitched them. It's because the mermaid is a mirror, and they see their true nature in her. They're not bewitched by the mermaid but set free.

SB: I really enjoyed your spin on mermaids and how unique it is from a "little"
tale we all know so well. Speaking of, it's no secret you love fairy tales. What are some of your favourites and why?

KR: When people think of fairy tales, true love and happy endings often come to mind, but I like my fairy tales Brothers Grimm style. I prefer fairy tales that are dark and brutal, where pain exists but so does healing. Fairy tales spark something primal and universal inside us. We can all relate to the fear of being abandoned, the injustice of being treated cruelly, or the misery of having a wicked stepmother.

Fairy tales make magic accessible to common people, and ordinary objects become powerful vessels. I love when humans can change their worlds with mirrors, hag stones, and pumpkins.

There are so many good fairy tales out there, but I'll try to name a few of my favourites. Hansel and Gretel because the evil witch is burned alive in the oven. Ashputtel because birds peck out her stepsisters' eyes. The Little Mermaid because she becomes a daughter of the air when she decides not to kill the prince. And Sweetheart Roland because a girl transforms herself and her lover into a beautiful swan and lake to escape the evil witch.

# Raspberry Buns

## Ingredients:

- 8 ounces self-raising flour
- 4 ounces of margarine
- 3 ounces of granulated sugar or caster sugar
- 1/4 cup of milk
- 1 tablespoon of vanilla extract
- 1 egg, beaten
- 1 cup of shredded coconut
- 4 tablespoons of raspberry jam

## Instructions:

- Set oven to 400 degrees F
- Grease and flour your baking sheet
- Sift the flour into a bowl and rub in the margarine
- Add the sugar, coconut flakes, and the beaten egg, then slowly add the milk
- Divide the mixture into small balls and place on your baking sheet
- Make a small hole in the center of each ball and spoon in the rasberry jam
- Bake for 10 minutes, then reduce heat to 350 degrees F and bake for 3-5 more minutes until buns are golden brown

# Pumpkin Soul Cakes

## Ingredients:

- 1/2 cup of vegetable or coconut oil
- 1 cup of whole milk
- 2 eggs
- 1 can of pumpkin puree
- 1 cup of brown sugar & 1/2 cup of granulated sugar
- 1 teaspoon of vanilla extract
- 2 teaspoons of cinnamon
- 1 teaspoon of nutmeg
- 1/2 teaspoon of cloves & 1/2 teaspoon of sea salt
- 3 teaspoons of baking powder
- 3 cups of all-purpose flour
- 1/2 cup of raisins & 1/2 cup of white chocolate chips

## Instructions:

- Set oven to 400 degrees F
- Line your baking sheet with parchment paper and spray with non-sticking baking spray
- Whisk eggs in a bowl, then add oil, milk, pumpkin puree, sugars, spices, salt, vanilla, and baking powder, then whisk ingredients well
- Add flour and smooth out the batter
- For each cake, pour enough batter to fill 1/4 cup, then mold the batter into a ball on the baking sheet
- Bake for about 10-14 minutes

# Lamb & Bean Stew

## Ingredients:

- 3-4 pounds of boneless lamb shoulder
- 2-3 cups of beef or chicken broth
- 1/2 an onion, chopped
- 1 zucchini, chopped
- 1 can of white beans (cannellini or navy), drained and rinsed
- 3 cloves of garlic, minced
- 1 teaspoon of thyme
- 1 teaspoon of rosemary

## Instructions:

- Place all the ingredients, except for the lamb and beans, in the slow cooker
- Then place the lamb in the slow cooker
- Turn slow cooker on low and cook for about 4-7 hours until the lamb is cooked through and can easily be pulled apart
- Place beans in the slow cooker for the last 30-40 minutes until they cook through
- Cooking times vary, so make sure the lamb is cooked through

# Spiced Brew

## Ingredients:

- 1-2 bottles of red wine
- 1 cup of cranberry juice
- 1 cup of cranberries
- 2 blood oranges or oranges, sliced
- 5 cinnamon sticks
- 2 teaspoons of cloves
- 2 cups of sugar
- 2 cups of blackberries
- 1 cup of blackberry simple syrup

## Instructions:

- To make blackberry simple syrup, place 1 cup of water, 1 cup of sugar, 2 cinnamon sticks, and 2 cups of blackberries in a saucepan on medium heat. As blackberries soften, mash them to release the flavor. Usually takes about 10-15 minutes. Then strain mixture into small bowl and discard the berries. Then set bowl aside.
- Turn crockpot on high and fill with wine, cranberry juice, cranberries, blood oranges, 3 cinnamon sticks, 1 cup of sugar, cloves, and 1 cup of blackberry simple syrup.
- Cook on high for one hour. Then turn down to low for 2-3 hours before serving.

www.ingramcontent.com/pod-product-compliance
Lightning Source LLC
Chambersburg PA
CBHW060543310726
48982CB00009B/1362/J

* 9 7 9 8 9 8 6 4 1 4 1 2 6 *